SWEETHEART COTTAGE

(A Cranberry Bay Book #1)

by

MINDY HARDWICK

ISBN: 978-0692542828

Cover Design by MK McClintock
Edited by Bev Katz Rosenbaum and Clare Wood
Formatted by Self-Publishing Services LLC. (www.self-publishing-service.com)

Eagle Bay Press
Lake Stevens, Washington

EAGLE BAY PRESS

For those who take the bet and risk the chance to love

Table of Contents

Acknowledgements   5

Chapter One   6

Chapter Two   16

Chapter Three   29

Chapter Four   40

Chapter Five   50

Chapter Six   60

Chapter Seven   74

Chapter Eight   89

Chapter Nine   99

Chapter Ten   111

Chapter Eleven   125

Chapter Twelve   134

Chapter Thirteen   142

Chapter Fourteen   152

Chapter Fifteen   166

Chapter Sixteen   175

Chapter Seventeen   186

Chapter One of *Weaving Magic*   196

Acknowledgements

This story's setting never would have been written without the inspiration of the north Oregon coast towns of Wheeler and Nehalem. Thank you for sharing your beautiful towns with me.

It takes a team to bring a book to publication and SWEETHEART COTTAGE is without exception. Thank you to the fabulous developmental editing of Bev Katz Rosenbaum and copyeditor, Clare Wood. Danica Winters and her team at SPS brought this story to readers faster and more efficiently than I ever dreamed possible.

As always, the Seattle RWA Chapter is invaluable to my growth as a writer and encourages me to take new risks and explore new options.

Thank you to my very best writer pal, Rhay Christou, whose emails and calls talk me off the ledge on a regular basis. Thank you to Mimi Fox at Mimi's A Shabby Chic Country Boutique for giving me the final push to start the ball rolling on this series. And, thank you to Dave Swords, whose mail I collected during a cold January which made me stay home with my butt in the chair and get this story written.

And especially thank you to my sweet contemporary readers who with their support and belief in my romantic storytelling encouraged me to start a new series.

Chapter One

A gust of wind threatened to shove Rylee's car off the Oregon highway and down the steep cliff to the forest below. She tightened her grip on the steering wheel and sang loudly with her favorite country-and-western singer, trying to drown out her increasing fears about the trip to Cranberry Bay.

Rylee slowed to peer at a small blue sign that pointed to a rest stop tucked into the backside of the mountain. She checked the rearview mirror. Her black-white-and-tan mutt, Raisin, stood on a threadbare towel in the backseat. He whined and pressed his nose to the glass. Rylee turned on her left blinker and slowed to exit.

"We'll get out of this storm," she said to the dog, more to reassure herself than Raisin. Rylee frowned at the small GPS attached to the dashboard. It hadn't picked up a signal to Cranberry Bay for miles, and she hoped it wasn't broken. She hadn't been back to the small town in ten years, not since she left Bryan. Rylee bit her lower lip and pushed away the thoughts of leaving her childhood sweetheart the morning after he proposed. She tried to focus on driving down the dark and rainy mountain road, where nothing looked the same as she remembered.

A small headache pounding between her eyes, Rylee followed the signs to the rest stop, pulling off the freeway onto a long ramp. She stopped in front of a brown, wood-shingled building. Picnic tables and a path curved down a hill toward a rushing stream. Towering evergreen trees surrounded the open green space. Signs pointed toward men's and women's restrooms. There wasn't another car in the parking lot, but a light glowed from a middle window in the building.

"Okay, bud," Rylee said. "It's going to be wet." She smiled at her faithful companion, who had ridden with her on the hundred-mile trip from Vegas. She didn't doubt Raisin understood rainstorms. She'd found him huddled against a Dumpster in the back alley outside her condo. It hadn't taken much to coax him inside; the leftover bite of her turkey sandwich was enough. Raisin became her only confidante as she packed up and sold everything off. Rylee's stomach twisted as she thought about the text she received from her partner and former best friend. Ericka had eloped with Rylee's fiancé and wanted out of their shared business immediately. Rylee was left with nothing but maxed out credit cards and rent on an expensive storefront. Only the letter she received from her grandmother's lawyer had given her any hope.

Rylee opened the car door, and the wind rushed through her short cardigan, thin lace shirt and cropped pants. She blasted the car heater to take away the mountain chill. None of the black pumps, skirts, and thin blouses inside her old, beat-up suitcase would be any warmer. But it didn't matter. She planned a quick sale of her grandmother's place. Once she convinced her gambling father to leave Vegas, something she knew he'd do as soon as he realized she was leaving him, she'd be on her way to San Diego to restart her life.

Rylee shivered and pulled her black cardigan tighter. Rain dripped against the side of her face as she stepped out of the car. A gust of wind blew strands of her hair against her mouth, and she pushed them aside and opened the backdoor. Rylee clipped on a leash and guided Raisin out of the car. The wind tossed Raisin's ears as he shook-off of the last five hours of travel. The trees above her head swayed, and Rylee quickly stepped away. A large branch could easily damage her car or hurt her.

Rylee hurried to the warmly lit building. She stepped under the covered porch. A coffee pot sat on a ledge beside a basket of napkins. A couple of dollar bills were stuffed inside a yellow coffee cup plastered with a black smiley face. A small handwritten sign said: "Donations Accepted."

"Cup of coffee, my dear?" A round-faced woman with deep-set blue eyes peered back at her from the other side of an open glass window. A basket of sewing yarns, threads, and measuring tapes was perched by her feet, and an old pair of jeans rested across her lap.

"Yes, please." Rylee reached in her pocket and pulled out a crumpled dollar bill. She dropped it in the donation cup and poured a thick stream of rich black coffee into a Styrofoam cup.

"Stormy evening." The woman pushed a plate of white-frosted oatmeal cookies toward Rylee.

Rylee shook her head at the cookies. "No, thank you." She barely had the dollar donation for the coffee. She didn't need cookies too.

"Go on," the woman's soothing voice wrapped around Rylee like a hug. "The chocolate-chip oatmeal cookies are my homemade special."

A deep ache dove through Rylee's chest. Grandma always made cookies for her when she arrived in Cranberry Bay for her summer childhood visits. Peanut-butter, chocolate-chip, and oatmeal cookies waited for her inside a colorful, old-fashioned tin that once belonged to Rylee's Great-Grandma. Rylee made a mental note to find her grandmother's tins. She planned to tuck a few things into her car before everything was marked to sell in the estate sale.

"Thank you." Rylee took a cookie from the tray and bit into it. The sweetness filled her mouth. It tasted exactly like her grandmother's recipe.

"I'm Beth Dawson. I run the coffee program at the rest stop for Cranberry Bay Community Youth. All the donations go toward helping youth attend a local summer camp where they can learn to swim, fish, and enjoy hiking."

"That's nice," Rylee muttered, not wanting to give away her own connections with Cranberry Bay. She was there only to sell her grandmother's house, and then she'd be on her way. Well-meaning strangers only threatened her family's longtime rule of not revealing her father's gambling secret. It was a secret they had kept since her father left town in his twenties, headed to a career as a minor league baseball player. The baseball career never materialized, and her father drifted into a twenty-year addiction with gambling. Years later, still unable to tell the town the truth about their famed hometown hero, Rylee had been driven out of Cranberry Bay and away from Bryan by her father's secret. She didn't need a reminder written on her calendar to remember to keep to herself during this trip.

"Do you have a pen?" Beth asked. "I'll write down the name of the camp. We accept donations all year-round. We're always looking for businesses to sponsor the kids."

Rylee fiddled in her purse for a pen. Once she got to San Diego and secured her job, she'd send a check to cover at least three kids. Giving back was a part of her business plan and something she made sure to include on her yearly goal chart. After all, Cranberry Bay was a town she always enjoyed visiting as a child.

Beth quickly wrote down the name of the camp and a website. "Here you go." Hope filled Beth's eyes. "Please. It's really important to these kids that they have a chance. If there is a business that is looking for a place to donate, we'd love to talk to them. We also love for people to volunteer. That's just as important as the money donation. Maybe if you have time…"

Abruptly, Rylee took the pen from Beth. The blue-and-green company emblem plastered to the side of it taunted her with everything she had lost. "I'll keep the camp in mind for a donation."

Tucking the piece of paper in her purse, Rylee walked over to the trash can, where she promptly dumped the pen and all reminders of her former life. Impatiently, she tugged on Raisin's leash and strode back to her car with the dog trotting behind her.

Quickly, she loaded Raisin into the backseat. Rylee slipped into the driver's seat and fiddled with the GPS buttons on her dashboard. The screen remained blank. Rylee frowned and pulled out of the parking lot. It couldn't be that much farther to Cranberry Bay. There should be signs pointing her in the right direction. Rylee breathed in and out. She hoped to arrive to Cranberry Bay before dark.

Rain pounded on the roof and a large semi-truck passed in the other lane. Water sprayed over her windshield as she slowed to avoid hydroplaning into the truck's lane. Rylee peered through the windshield and searched for a road sign telling her she needed to turn off the highway to reach Cranberry Bay. She didn't remember much about the trip when Grandma and Grandpa used to pick her up at the Portland airport. After Mom died, Dad always made sure to send her to

Cranberry Bay for the entire summer. Both of them pretended they didn't know Dad would spend the summer in the casinos. She loved those childhood summer days when daylight stretched far into the evening. By the time she was nineteen, she and her childhood sweetheart, Bryan, had declared their love for each other. Even now, her insides warmed as she remembered how he made her feel—loved, cherished, and protected. The night he proposed, she believed everything would finally work out. She would find a way for Dad to get help for his addiction. He could return to Cranberry Bay and enjoy his life again. But the next morning, everything had crashed when the Vegas police called. She left immediately, knowing she could never leave her father alone in Vegas, and he couldn't return to Cranberry Bay until he was the hometown hero they all remembered and loved. But ten years later, her father was still gambling, Bryan had married someone else, both her grandparents were dead, and she had just lost the only thing she had left in the world—her career.

A blast of wind blew across the highway, and Rylee swerved to avoid missing a small branch. Raisin let out a sharp bark and paced back and forth on the backseat. A small tire light on the dash flashed, and the car bumped with a flat. Rylee cursed and steered toward a small gravel pullout. In the summer, motor homes and slow-moving cars stopped to allow streams of cars pass. Now there was no one on the gravel road. Rylee drove alongside a small trailhead and parked.

Twenty-four hours before she left Vegas, Rylee had traded in her gorgeous black Lexus for an old, four-door car with the large dent on the left side. The dealer told her the used car needed new tires. She had a budget for how long she could make her meager savings account last. New car tires were not in the budget.

Rylee reached over to the passenger seat and fumbled inside her brown leather purse. She'd simply call her emergency roadside assistance number for help. Rylee unzipped her purse and pulled out her phone, only to see the small message in the window: "No service." That explained the GPS problem.

Hold it together, she told herself as panic rose in her chest. She could handle the situation. The enclave of trees must be blocking the reception. She would simply walk back to the rest stop and ask Beth for help. It had to be less than a mile back down the road. She could walk a mile. On her treadmill, she walked at least three miles a day. Of course, it wasn't in the middle of a windstorm, and she always wore her expensive sports shoes during her workouts, not her flimsy open-toed black sandals. But those were just details.

Rylee peered outside the window. She longed for the small blue emergency bag Grandma and Grandpa tucked into the backseat of their car. As a child, Rylee loved to explore the blue bag and check for the white candles, matches, flashlight, extra batteries, flares, granola bars, water jug, and the thick maroon blanket. One summer, she created an entire spreadsheet of the items in the blue bag and gave it to her grandparents. They tucked the paper inside the front pocket for safekeeping.

She pressed her nose to the window. If she walked against the traffic on the left side of the road, she could do it. "Come on, bud," Rylee said to Raisin. "We're going for a little walk."

Rylee stepped out of the car as headlights rounded the bend and splayed into her eyes. She lifted her hand to shield her vision from the glaring lights. A tree branch cracked behind her and landed somewhere close by with a thud. She didn't need her list of goals to tell her she had to get out of here. Fast.

The small truck slowed, and Rylee's heart pounded. The only person who expected her was her grandparents' lawyer, and her appointment was on Monday morning. There wasn't a person in Vegas who cared where she was, and, except for Beth Dawson, she hadn't talked to anyone in days. By the time someone realized she was missing, it'd be too late for anyone to find her.

Rylee scurried into the passenger seat and locked the doors. "Now would be a good time for you to bark," Rylee said, turning around and looking at Raisin. Of course, he wasn't barking, unlike the last five days where she'd done her best to keep him from barking at slamming doors and suitcases being lugged up and down stairs in the hotels.

The blue sports pickup maneuvered in front of her car. A colorful sticker, plastered on the back bumper, said: "Doug Mays for Cranberry Bay Mayor." A tall, broad-shouldered man stepped out of the truck. He wore jeans and heavy brown hiking boots and strode purposefully toward Rylee's car. Rain cascaded off his thick hooded black jacket. He tapped briefly on her window. "Everything okay?" he mouthed. "It's a nasty storm out here."

"I have a flat."

The man raised an eyebrow and shook his head.

He couldn't hear her. She'd have to take her chances and roll down the window. Thanking the age of her car, Rylee turned the old-fashioned window crank and yelled above the wind, "My left front tire is flat."

"I'll take a look. Do you have a spare?"

"In the trunk. I can help you..." She knew how to change a tire. She didn't need this man to rescue her.

"I got it," the man hollered. "It's nasty out here. I'm already soaked. Stay there."

Rylee nodded. It was pouring rain, and she wasn't exactly dressed for changing a tire. Raisin paced on the backseat, and Rylee reached into his treat bag on the front seat. She held the small dog biscuit out to Raisin, and he gobbled it from her hand.

A sharp tap on the car window jerked Rylee's attention away from Raisin. The man's hood had fallen off, and his blond hair was wet. Rylee swallowed hard. Her eyes passed over his high forehead and the freckles that danced across his cheekbones. A flicker of recognition crossed his face at the same time as her heart fluttered. Bryan gazed back at her with all the kindness and compassion she once remembered.

Slowly, Rylee stepped out of the car as Raisin gave a sharp bark in the backseat. "It's okay, boy," Rylee said to Raisin. She pressed her hands against the back of the car and leaned against it, trying to steady herself. The wet car soaked the back of her bare legs, but she barely felt it. Rain fell off her head and danced onto the gravel below her feet.

"Bryan," Rylee whispered. Her insides quivered from something that reached into her far deeper than the cold rain and wind. She didn't dare look at his hand to see the gold wedding band that claimed him as belonging to someone else. She tried to steady herself. She'd known it was a possibility to run into Bryan; Cranberry Bay wasn't that big. But nothing could have prepared her heart for the moment when it actually happened.

Bryan's eyes swept over her face, down her soaking wet cardigan, and to her red painted toenails peeking from the tips of her sandals. "Rylee?" A shadow flashed across his face. "I thought it was you...but I didn't..."

Suddenly he cleared his throat. "Pop the trunk, and I'll get that spare on for you."

Rylee nodded and slipped into the driver's seat. She leaned down and lifted the trunk latch. Her hands shook as the old feelings for Bryan rushed through her.

Chapter Two

Bryan rolled under beside the car and positioned the spare tire in place. He lifted the tire onto the axle and gave it a hard twist, ensuring it was snug. A heavy lock of wet hair fell to his forehead, and he brushed it aside. Memories poured through his mind. Rylee sitting on the front porch swing, painting her toes red, and smiling at him. Rylee and her soft mouth that he couldn't stop kissing. Rylee, who had told him she loved him and promised to marry him, but left the next day, leaving his heart in pieces.

When the spare was firmly in place, Bryan rolled out from under the car. He walked to the driver's side.

Rylee rolled down the window, and he cleared his throat. "That should hold you until you get into Cranberry Bay. I'm sorry about your grandmother. Cranberry Bay will miss her."

"Thank you," Rylee said. "I always planned to return to see her. But I kept putting it off, things came up…" Rylee's voice softened to barely a whisper.

"Yes, well…" Bryan shifted and looked away from her and into the tall evergreens. Rain bounced off his shoulders and landed on the ground with soft splats. He wasn't sure if he was angry with himself for believing Rylee's words now or for the years he held on to the foolish belief that she'd come back to him and Cranberry Bay. He had tried everything he could to forget her, including marrying someone he didn't love. Nothing had worked.

"I imagine you won't find Cranberry Bay any different." Bryan repeatedly opened and closed his left hand. He quickly pocketed his hand and ran his finger over his empty ring finger. Nothing had changed in Cranberry Bay over the last ten years. Jobs were scarce and limited to clamming, forestry, and dairy farming. Summer tourists streamed past on the freeway, stopping only to grab an iced coffee or browse the antique shop before heading into the popular surrounding beach towns. Cranberry Bay was a stop for lunch on the way to somewhere else.

"I'm not planning to stay long. I'll clean out the house, sell it, and then I'm moving to San Diego," Rylee said firmly.

Bryan couldn't help but smile, faintly. Rylee was still the same, making plans for her life to run according to a set schedule. It'd been one of the things he loved about her. Every summer, she outlined a plan of hikes she wanted to take, crafts she wanted to make, and meals she wanted to cook. By the end of the summer, her plan was always complete. The only summer it hadn't been was the summer they fell in love. Instead of working through her plan, they'd spent long lazy days floating on the river and evenings exploring each other in the small river cottage. He often teased her about her summer plan, and she only smiled and said sometimes plans changed. He had loved nothing better than knowing he was a part of that plan-changing summer. If only it could have been forever.

"Thank you for fixing the tire." Rylee raised her eyes and met Bryan's. His heart pounded in his chest, the same way it always had when she looked at him, making him believe he had more to offer than he ever believed in himself. She'd always had that ability. A way to look at him or touch his arm and convince him he could do anything.

"Rylee..." Bryan cleared his throat. There was so much he wanted to say to her. But a gust of wind blew into the trees above their head, and a large branch cracked. "Cranberry Bay is about ten-miles from here. Stay straight on the highway and I'll follow you into Cranberry Bay. The storm is pretty bad."

"Thank you," Rylee said and rolled up her window.

Slowly, she pulled out of the gravel and onto the highway.

Bryan strode to his truck and slipped inside. His pulse raced as a large tree branch dropped to the ground where Rylee's car had been parked. He put his truck in gear and pulled onto the highway. Mountain storms in the fall were not things to play with. His younger brother, Adam, worked as a forest ranger and had more than one harrowing story about a hiker who'd gotten trapped by falling trees.

Bryan flipped off the mystery audiobook he had been listening to and turned the station to rock. The heavy drumbeat filled his ears as he followed Rylee's car down the mountain highway. One of Rylee's taillights flickered and turned off. He made a mental note to fix that for her as soon as possible and hoped Sheriff Anderson was off-duty tonight. The sheriff looked for ways to make money and didn't think twice of ticketing cars for missing taillights. Bryan had gotten a few tickets himself, but he usually managed to finagle his way out of them by buying a couple rounds of microbrews at the pub.

Slowing to twenty-five, Bryan drove past the river marina in the gloom. A few fishing boats were tethered to the docks, and the pub lights glowed as the music of one of the popular beach bands poured through the open doors. They spent the off-season practicing new songs at the pub. Bryan sometimes grabbed his own guitar and joined in. He liked spending the long, dark, rainy evenings with many of the men whom he had known all his life.

Across from the marina, the city park overlooked the bay, and wooden benches dripped with rain. Heavy dark leaves covered the grass. In the fading light, the chipped paint on the buildings and the overgrown grass wasn't noticeable. Bryan worked with a crew of high school kids to keep things tidy. The teens earned volunteer credits, and the city enjoyed a well-kept summer park. Once school started, he did the job with occasional help from a teen on a Saturday.

Ahead of him, Rylee made a left on Elm Street and her taillight faded out of sight. Bryan turned right, two streets away from Rylee's grandmother's house, and continued past the town's two-story, brick elementary school and the gymnasium in the playground that his Dad had helped build years ago. The PTA never had funding to replace the old set with a new one, and a couple of the swings were missing. Half a block past the playground, Bryan turned left onto an asphalt-paved driveway. He slowly pulled up behind the Jeep Grand Cherokee belonging to his older brother, Sawyer, and the four-door black Honda CRV belonging to his younger brother, Adam. The garage door stood open, and his Mom's small, silver Toyota was nestled inside beside a shelving unit filled with plastic bins of Christmas decorations.

The home was like the other two-story Craftsman homes on the street. When he was eleven, Dad hired a couple guys to build a dormer on the back. Dad joked about never being able to get the loan paid off before he retired, but six months after the dormer was finished,

Dad suddenly passed away of a heart attack. His generous life-insurance policy not only paid off the dormer but also the rest of the mortgage, giving Rebecca Shuster and her two boys and her twins a place to call home, worry-free.

Bryan kicked aside large piles of leaves as he headed up the walkway. The gingham living room curtains stood open, and golden lamplight blazed into the dark and rainy night. A steady trail of water drained off the roof into a large puddle. He made a mental note to stop by and check the gutter tomorrow. A large pine tree hung over the house and dropped needles onto the roof. The needles easily clogged the gutters and caused damage to the cedar siding if left unchecked.

A glowing carved pumpkin sat on the front porch step, and Bryan smiled. Yesterday, when he stopped by to see about a leaky toilet in the downstairs bathroom, the pumpkin hadn't been carved. Tonight, candlelight shone from a stenciled nose, mouth, and pair of lopsided eyes. A plastic carving tool lay across the front porch by the pumpkin. Bryan leaned down and picked up the knife.

He opened the front door, and the smell of pot roast wafted through the room, which was painted bright yellow. A fire crackled in the fireplace, and Adam leaned against the stone mantel.

"We were ready to eat without you." Adam's dark, thick heavy hair lay across his forehead in a mass of curls. He wore dark jeans and a flannel shirt, unbuttoned three buttons so his white undershirt poked through. He'd kicked off his usual heavy boots, and his large feet in black-and-gray flannel socks shifted on the hardwood floor.

"Sorry I'm late." Bryan said. "It was a long trip back from Portland."

Sawyer uncrossed his legs and stood up from a plush, leather reclining chair. He drained the last of his beer and nodded to Brian. "There are more drinks in the fridge."

"Thanks," Bryan said. "I think I'll go see if Mom needs any help." Sawyer had never been a big drinker, but ever since his beloved wife had died of cancer, he had a habit of making sure there was enough alcohol flowing to keep the pain away.

It didn't surprise Bryan to find both his brothers lounging in the living room while Mom cooked dinner. After Dad died, each brother played a different part in the family. He helped Mom in the house. Sawyer contributed money when Mom needed a little extra, and Adam helped by driving Mom the hour-and-a-half over the mountains to Portland for appointments and shopping trips to purchase bulk household items. It was unspoken between the three of them that they would take care of Mom.

Bryan kicked off his mud-splattered shoes and left them lying at the front door with Adam's work boots. A small pair of pink tennis shoes lay, upside down, on top of Sawyer's dress shoes. He smiled at his niece Lauren's haphazard way of making sure her Dad didn't forget to take her home, too. Not that Sawyer had any thought of leaving his daughter behind. He loved her fiercely and would do anything for his little girl.

Bryan's socked feet padded against the hardwood floor as he passed the wall in the hallway filled with family photos. Bryan's left shoulder brushed against a small gold frame and tilted the picture. In the picture, he and his twin sister, Lisa, stood by a green canoe that was alongside a river. Lisa was the only one of the Shuster siblings who had left Cranberry Bay. She had married a fisherman from Seattle and took a job working as a public relations director at a children's hospital. A few years into the marriage, Frank died at sea during a fishing trip to Alaska, leaving Lisa to raise their daughter, Maddie. She often declined invitations to come home at the holidays, saying she was needed too much by the families at the hospital. Bryan understood Lisa's commitment to her work, but he missed his twin and niece and wished they lived closer.

Bryan averted his eyes from the last picture on the wall. A framed photo of Dad and his sister and brothers gathered in a large circle around a canoe. Bryan stood a small distance away from all of them with a scowl on his face. The camping trip had been only one more time he didn't please Dad.

Bryan headed into the kitchen where Mom chopped plump tomatoes at a wooden cutting board beside the sink. Lauren perched on a stool and dropped pieces of lettuce into salad bowls. She wore jeans and a blue sweatshirt with Eagles stenciled across the front. Clasped in a high ponytail, her curly blonde hair swung with every move.

"Let me do that, Mom." Bryan stepped up behind her and took the knife out of her hands. "We'll finish up, right Lauren?"

Lauren hopped down from the stool. She pushed her bangs out of her eyes, but they flopped back down in the same place again. "Grandma let me carve the pumpkin today."

"I know." Bryan held up the plastic knife. "You left the knife on the porch."

"Sorry!" Lauren jumped over and yanked the utensil from Bryan's hand. She twirled across the kitchen, opened the pantry door, and dropped it into the trash can.

Rebecca grabbed a red-and-blue hot pad, and, opening the oven, pulled out the steaming pot roast. She carried it to the counter and set it on a hot plate. "I think we're all set." Rebecca wiped her hands on an orange-and-black ruffled apron. She nodded toward the dining room table, set with the family's blue-and-white dinnerware set.

"Smells great." Sawyer strolled into the kitchen and ruffled his daughter's hair. "Time to put the ice in the glasses," he instructed her.

Obediently, Lauren opened the lower freezer drawer and pulled out the bin of ice. She grabbed a set of plastic tongs and headed into the dining room.

Sawyer dropped his empty bottle of beer into the recycling bin by the backdoor and looked into the dark backyard. "How's business, Bryan?" Sawyer whirled around, and his brown eyes met Bryan's. "Sold any houses yet?"

"I'm working on it." Bryan fisted his hands. Eight years ago, Sawyer had gotten a lucky break when he was hired to be the developer of a premier community at the beach. The houses sold quickly, but instead of continuing to buy property, Sawyer bought ten acres on the outskirts of town and built his own home. During the housing crash, Sawyer had money in the bank and nothing in land. While developers around him fell, Sawyer slowly bought up property at rock bottom prices. Now, he owned what seemed like half the county and had accounts large enough to buy another country estate, something he never stopped reminding Bryan, who hadn't been as lucky as his older brother in business.

Rebecca reached behind her and untied her apron. "Jack mentioned he's handling Ellen Harper's estate for her granddaughter, Rylee. I suspect they will need a real estate agent for the sale."

She smiled at Bryan. Jack Perkins had been a longtime family friend. A widow for the last five years, he and Rebecca spent more and more time together. Both of them waved off all discussion of romance.

"Rylee Harper." Sawyer leaned against the counter. He crossed his arms over his chest and studied Bryan. "Kinda remember you wanted to marry her…"

"Yes." Bryan grabbed a plate, loaded it with roast beef, and carried it to the table. "Childhood fantasy." He pulled out a chair and sat down beside Adam, hoping Sawyer would let the conversation drop.

"She might have made the best decision to leave Cranberry Bay." Sawyer moved a heavy oak chair, straightening the paisley cushion. He sat down opposite him. "The School Board is talking about closing the elementary school and sending the kids to the coast elementary, twenty miles away."

"Closing the elementary school?" Bryan dropped his fork to the plate with a thud. How could they close the elementary school and tear it down? The school hosted annual carnival fund-raisers, children's art workshops, and community education classes on everything from cooking to hiking to dog training. If the school was closed and torn down, everything would stop. There was nowhere else in the town big enough to hold the community events.

"Shh…" Sawyer raised his finger to his lips as Lauren danced into the dining room. She balanced her plate in one hand and a glass of milk in the other.

"Probably won't happen right away," Sawyer said, eying Lauren as she sank into a chair on the other side of him. "But people are concerned. Families are dwindling, and the school has lost a lot of funding without the tax base here. The district thinks it'd be better to combine some schools."

Bryan picked up his napkin and set it in his lap. "I might have a solution for Cranberry Bay." He took a bite of his salad as his brothers turned to him. Bryan smiled, enjoying the moment of attention from his family. Most of the time, it was his brothers who held the center stage, not him.

"And..." Adam asked, scooping a heaping spoonful of mashed potatoes onto his plate.

"I met with a seller in Portland today. He's selling a couple of riverboats. A casino and a hotel. I'd like to buy them and begin to bring tourism back to Cranberry Bay. If we could build up our travel and tourism revenue, we'd be able to offer jobs and be eligible for some of the state tax money that the beach towns enjoy. We could be much more than a stop-through on the way to somewhere else, if we had something for people to do and a reason to stay for a night or two."

"That's a fabulous idea." Ellen leaned over and set a steaming bowl of vegetables on the table. She took her seat at the head of the table and briefly smiled at each of the brothers and Lauren.

"Have you talked to the bank about securing a loan?" Adam asked. "I've heard it's still hard to get financing for commercial real estate."

"The lending restrictions are still tight." Bryan ran his fingers over the etched glass filled with water. He didn't tell his brothers that his own lack of a steady job history, combined with not owning his own home hadn't won him any points at the bank. A few years ago, during his divorce, he'd given everything to Amy, knowing the reason for their marriage failing was his inability to let go of Rylee Harper. Amy had immediately sold the house and moved to Portland, where he heard she'd remarried and had two children.

"I'm hoping to gather some funding from people who might be interested in sponsoring the project."

Sawyer lowered his fork and studied Bryan. "Funding isn't going to be easy to find in Cranberry Bay. Most people can barely keep the lights on."

Bryan fisted his left hand at his side. Sawyer's words traveled to his gut and stuck there, like something he'd eaten that hadn't agreed with him. "You got any other options?"

"It sounds like a worthwhile proposition, and one I might be interested in funding. But..."

"But..." Bryan gazed at Sawyer, feeling as if he'd been hurled back to their years of childhood board-game nights where Sawyer always won. Game shark, the family called him. Everything was a game to Sawyer, and nine times out of ten, he won.

"But you know how I like a game..."

Bryan's stomach clenched. He knew all too well about Sawyer's bets. He'd watched him over the years offer bets to people and laugh about them when they lost. But he was running out of options and time quickly. "What is your game this time?"

"I'll give you the full funding for the riverboats, but..." Sawyer paused and eyed him, obviously relishing in the power he held over his younger brother, "you have to convince Rylee Harper to move to Cranberry Bay. She can sell her grandmother's home or not. But she has to decide she loves Cranberry Bay so much that she'll live here full time. If you can convince Rylee to move to Cranberry Bay, then I will know you can convince anyone to move here."

"And, how do you propose I do that?" Bryan asked, pressure building in his stomach at the thought of Rylee

Harper living in Cranberry Bay for good. She'd never agree to it, and if she did, how would he handle seeing her everyday around town? He had barely been able to contain his emotions at seeing her on the dark and wet highway. The town was too small for them not to bump into each other on a regular basis.

Sawyer leaned back in his chair. "That is up to you to figure out."

Bryan licked his lips. His mouth tasted dry. "You know Rylee and I are never going to be together. That's over." The words felt like lies on his tongue, and he forced them out. He and Rylee were over. She'd made that clear the morning he found her note telling him she'd returned to Las Vegas. He'd tried to contact her a couple times, but each time, her phone went only to voice mail. As the weeks turned into months, his hope of her returning dwindled, and, finally, he'd done the only thing he knew how to do to get over her; He married someone else. The marriage had lasted only eighteen months, and he had never forgotten Rylee Harper.

Sawyer bit into a small tomato. He shrugged. "I don't really care what you and Rylee Harper do or don't do."

"Then why are you setting up this bet about her?"

"Because..." Sawyer placed his hands on the table and leaned forward, "I'd offer you the money, but I know you'll never take it without a challenge. You like the challenge, and Rylee Harper is the best challenge I see right now. She is the perfect candidate for convincing that Cranberry Bay has something to offer."

Bryan forked a piece of meat. His head pounded. He'd never win the bet. Rylee had no intention of staying in Cranberry Bay. She made that clear today. She had no more desire to stay in Cranberry Bay today than she did ten years ago when she left and broke his heart. But he also needed money. He needed a way to save Cranberry Bay and prove to the town and himself he could be what his Dad had claimed he couldn't be— a success. The bank wouldn't give him the loan, and time was ticking. If he didn't do something, the town that he'd grown up in, the people he cared about, and the place he loved would become nonexistent. He could not allow that to happen.

Lauren leaned over to him. "Are they closing my school? Please don't let them close it."

Bryan gazed into his niece's pleading eyes. She'd already lost so much when her Mom died of cancer; he couldn't allow her to lose her elementary school too. Not when he could do something to save the town.

Bryan jerked his head back up and stared at Sawyer. "Game on." He would find a way to convince Rylee Harper to stay without allowing his heart to be shattered.

Chapter Three

Rylee pulled up in front of her Grandparents' two-story bungalow. Rain poured off the roof and out of the gutters. An overturned set of lawn chairs lay haphazardly on the covered porch. A pile of wet wood leaned against a cedar fence beside the closed garage door. Grandpa had loved working on broken lawn mowers, bikes, and old cars, and he never shut the garage door. It was how she met Bryan, all those years ago. He'd been one of the many young men of Cranberry Bay whom Grandpa had mentored in the art of mechanics during their high school and college years. She stared at the dark house and swallowed a lump. Memories filled her mind of colorful red-and-white geraniums planted in large blue pots and an American flag flying on the porch.

Raisin whined from the backseat.

"Okay, bud. We're here." It was silly to think the house would resemble her childhood memories. The lawyer warned her that after her grandfather died, her grandmother hadn't been able to take care of the home. He told her things wouldn't look like she remembered. Rylee pulled out a small tablet of paper from her purse. She jotted down: Clean the gutter. Sweep the porch. Mow the lawn. Rylee tucked the small tablet into her purse as the tension in her shoulders eased with the organization of her list.

Rylee stepped out of the car, opened the backdoor, and clipped Raisin's leash to his collar. The dog hopped to the ground and shook himself. The trainer she'd taken Raisin to for a few lessons told her to look for the "shake-offs." A dog that had been abandoned often demonstrated signs of stress about riding in cars. The shake-off was a way of shaking off the stress. Rylee wanted to do her own shake off as she led Raisin through the overgrown front yard.

Raisin peed on a peeling porch post, and after he finished, Rylee tugged on his leash and headed up the front steps. She walked over a loose board and onto the wooden deck. The lawyer, Jack Perkins, hadn't given her a set of keys. He'd instructed her to stop by his office in town. But Rylee doubted he'd still be at his office on a dark and rainy fall evening. Most likely, he'd be at home eating dinner and enjoying a relaxing evening with family.

She took two steps to the left side of the porch, reached her hand underneath the rotted wooden beam, and found the plastic key box. Grandpa had installed the lockbox one summer during her visit. Her grandparents had needed to travel to Portland for the day to visit with a doctor. Rylee convinced them that, at age thirteen, she was old enough to stay home by herself. But when she left for the library, Rylee locked the door handle and forgot to take the set of keys. She spent the day reading stacks of books about starting a business. By four-o-clock, she was hungry and a light rain covered the sidewalks. By the time her grandparents arrived home, she'd fallen asleep, leaning against the porch railing. The next day, Grandpa walked to the local hardware store and bought a key box to install. He programmed the code to be her birthday, so she would always remember.

Rylee clicked the numbers on the box, and, with a little tug, lifted off the lid. She took the key out of the box and inserted it into the door. The door stuck, and she gave it a hard push with her shoulder. As she stepped inside, the smell of cat urine and raw sewage overpowered her. Rylee quickly grabbed her sweater and jerked the collar over her nose. She reached for the wall light switch and turned it to "On." Nothing happened. Rylee gritted her teeth. Of course the lights wouldn't work. No one had been paying the bills. Mentally, she added call the electric company and add her name to the billing, as well as call the gas company for heat onto her list of things to do.

Carefully, Rylee stretched her hand out and made her way through the darkened living room and into the hallway. She kept her fingers trailing along the wall as she moved slowly in the dark. A small bit of light from the street streamed in from the living room windows and gave her a bit of help in seeing her way. If she could reach the closet, Grandma always stored a box of storm supplies, including a radio, battery, and flashlights, inside a plastic bin in the closet. Suddenly, Rylee's hand felt the closet doorknob, and she pulled it open. The plastic tub lay in the same place it had always been, at the bottom. A stack of kitchen towels rested on top of the tub. Rylee pulled out a small hand towel and buried her face in it. The softness reminded her of Grandma, and the tears bubbled in her throat.

Raisin pressed his cold nose against Rylee's side. She reached down to pet him, and his soft fur calmed her. Rylee placed the towel on the floor and reached back into the closet. She flipped open the tub lid and grabbed the flashlight. Thankfully, the flashlight still had a small bit of charge, and a dim light bounced off the walls of the living room. A large water stain ran from the ceiling, down the wall, and to the floorboards. Parts of the ceiling plaster lay scattered across the floor.

Rylee clenched her teeth as she added to her list the growing number of items that needed repair.

Scurrying noises moved above her head, and Raisin barked sharply. Rylee shivered. Rats or raccoons? Raisin bolted up the stairs, panting and barking. "Raisin!" Rylee hollered. A raccoon could tear him apart. Rylee ran behind him and clutched the flashlight in front of her. She tried not to think about small critters jumping from ceiling beams and into her hair.

Raisin bolted into the bathroom and stopped at the edge of the tub. He barked twice. Rylee cautiously leaned over the porcelain. A calico cat with five kittens was tucked in the corner. The cat hissed and scrunched closer to the kittens. Rylee grabbed Raisin by the scruff of the neck and pushed him out of the bathroom.

"Stay," she said. Raisin sat on the hardwood floor and stared at her. He let out a small whine. His eyes pleaded with her. It was the same look he gave her when she allowed him to sleep on the bed with her. But this time, Rylee shook her head and shut the bathroom door. From the other side, she heard Raisin press against the door as he lay down beside it.

Cool air blew inside the small bathroom from the open window above the tub. Rylee sank to the old and faded bathroom mat. She leaned against the toilet and rested the flashlight on the floor. The dim light bounced off the full-length mirror attached to the back of the door. How had things derailed so badly? Ryle fingered the fringed bath rug. She'd followed all of the best practices in business and had risen to the top of the decorating world in Las Vegas. She traveled the world, scouring antique markets for just the right touch for her clients. She donated large amounts of money to various nonprofits all over the Vegas area, and she paid her father's constant gambling debts. She served on the

Chamber of Commerce Board and enjoyed elaborate parties and tickets to top name shows in Vegas. But none of it had mattered; her best friend had still run off with her half of the business and a man Rylee had once believed she could love more than she had once loved Bryan. That was something that, after seeing Bryan again, Rylee realized wasn't true. Her heart had never forgotten her first love, and she'd just been fooling herself.

A quiet meow came from inside the bathtub, and Rylee raised herself to her knees. She peered over the edge. A pair of dark black eyes stared back at her. "I bet you didn't plan for things to end up this way either, did you?"

A knock at the front door jolted Rylee to her feet. She grabbed the flashlight and quickly hurried down the stairs to the entryway. Her heart pounded. Who was visiting now? The residents of Cranberry Bay were a generous and supportive group, but on a rainy, stormy night like this, Rylee doubted any of them would have braved the storm to stop by for a cup of coffee.

At the front door, she pulled aside the dusty window curtains and peered outside. Bryan's kind smile beamed at her. He waved, and she pulled open the door.

"What are you doing here?" Rylee placed her hands on her hips and didn't move out of the way or invite him in.

"I was just finishing up our weekly family dinner." Bryan took a step back on the small porch. The smile vanished from his face. "I wanted to check if you needed anything." He peered beyond her into the dark house. "The lights aren't on?"

"The lights are not on," Rylee said, exhaling. "There is a family of cats in the upstairs bathroom, a leaking roof, water damage down the side of the living room wall, and the place smells like sewage." The story poured out of Rylee like the rushing river running alongside the town.

"Why don't I get some guys over here to take care of things in the morning? I know quite a few people in town who'd love to make a little extra cash."

"No," Rylee said. "I'll find a way to deal with it." She needed a little extra cash herself, and, even more importantly, she didn't want to run the risk of hiring someone who had been her Dad's friend and would question her about him. She didn't have answers for the town or herself as to how the town's superstar baseball player could dissolve into a gambling addict who lived on the streets of Vegas. "In the daylight, things will look better." She honestly couldn't imagine how things could look better in the light. Most likely, they would look worse.

"You can't stay here." Bryan peered into the darkness behind Rylee. "There aren't any lights and it's freezing. Why don't I show you the River Rock Inn? It's a gorgeous old place with rooms on the river. They have a couple rooms that are pet friendly." He stuck his hands in his pockets, and his eyes softened. "There's a good bakery right next door. Sasha, the owner makes the best turkey sandwiches and serves a strong coffee. She's usually open in the evenings. I'm headed over to the office to work a bit. The bakery and inn are right around the corner. Why don't you follow me in your car with Raisin?"

Rylee took a deep breath. There was no way she could pay for a night at the inn, but a sandwich did sound good. She'd have something to eat, and then return to the house to sleep. In the morning, things would look better.

"A sandwich sounds great." Rylee called Raisin to her side and grabbed her purse. "I'll follow you."

"Wait." Bryan shrugged out of his heavy raincoat. "It's cold out there. Take this. I've got another one at the office. I'll pick it up."

Rylee shook her head at his offer. "I'll grab something from the closet. I'm sure Grandma had a coat or two that will fit me." She turned around and opened the coat closet. The empty hangers hung in a row, and a small wadded up piece of gum wrapper lay on the floor. "Grandma didn't have any coats?"

"She gave them away," Bryan said. "Mom helped her with a huge garage sale last summer. I think she knew her time was short."

Rylee wrapped her arms around herself. Her insides shook. Her Grandma had known she didn't have long to live, but she hadn't called her to come back. Did Grandma not want to run the risk of calling her, knowing her father might also return and show the town who he'd become? Or did Grandma not want to risk asking her, knowing she'd declined all the other offers to return? Rylee had claimed important business commitments, which now seemed less important in the face of her death.

"Rylee?"

"Yes. Thank you." Rylee lifted the coat from Bryan's hand. She slipped into the coat and struggled to find the second sleeve.

Bryan stepped up behind her and lifted the coat, so she could slip her left arm inside. "It's a bit big, but it's warm and will keep the rain off you."

The aspen smell of his scent clung to the coat, and she pulled it tighter around her. Keep yourself together, she warned herself. She could not risk getting close to Bryan again. He didn't understand how loving someone

35

the way she had once loved him put everything she and her family had always kept in secret about her father in jeopardy. Bryan had a beautiful family whom he loved and who loved him. He and the rest of the town did not need to see her father standing on the street corner with a cardboard sign, begging for more money to gamble. Shame filled her as she thought of how often she'd found her father digging for food at one of the fast-food restaurant's Dumpsters. "Thank you. I'm sure it will be fine until tomorrow when I can get my own coat."

Bryan held open the front door. "After you."

Rylee stepped past him, and as she brushed against his solid chest, she felt his sharp intake of breath. Then the moment vanished, and she wondered if it had happened at all as they hustled down the walk and into separate cars.

Minutes later, Rylee drove her car slowly through the town's tree-lined streets. Wide sidewalks, Craftsman-style homes, and grassy front yards covered each block. On a nice day, she and Raisin could walk into town. But tonight, the wind blew the leaves across the pavement and small evergreen branches littered the sidewalks. Lights glowed from living room windows, and orange pumpkins sat on front porches. The smell of fireplace wood smoke drifted in through the car ventilators. All of it screamed to her of family and home, things she'd never had and pushed away as ever wanting for herself because they would always be out of her reach.

Bryan drove slowly, as if he was giving her a tour and allowing her all the time she wanted to take in the small town. As she passed each home, memories flooded Rylee. Memories of sitting on front porches with her grandparents, memories of walking with her Grandpa to town for an ice cream cone, and memories of stopping at the local hardware store to pick up a few things he needed.

On Main Street, Bryan pulled to a stop in front of a yellow, two-story building. Black shutters lined the windows and a small white light glowed from each room. A strand of white lights outlined a wooden sign with green letters hung above the front door, "River Rock Inn."

Rylee pulled her car behind Bryan's and stared at the warm lights inside the building. She wanted nothing more than to walk inside, check in, and go lie down on a thick cushioned bed and sleep for days. But she couldn't and, even more importantly, she couldn't tell Bryan each dollar left in her savings account was carefully accounted for until the sale of the house. She knew he would offer to pay for the night, and she couldn't allow him to do so.

Bryan stepped out of his car and walked to her window.

"Gracie serves an amazing breakfast in the morning. She buys the scones and breads from Sasha's bakery. I'm sure you'll enjoy it." Bryan smiled at her, unaware of the conflicting emotions racing inside her.

Rylee looked away from him. "I'm sure it's great."

"Everything okay?"

"Sure," Rylee said. "I'll just park here and check-in. You don't have to wait." Her voice sounded calm and steady. Lies to cover and smooth everything, something she'd learned watching her Dad work the creditors who called their home constantly. Of course, the biggest lie had been the one, unspoken, between them and her grandparents—the lie of her father's gambling, which kept all of them apart and unable to reach out for each other.

Bryan peered closely at her. "I'll be over at the office for a few hours if you need anything."

"What exactly do you do?" Rylee asked suddenly.

"I'm a real estate agent," Bryan said, and winked at her.

"A real estate agent?"

"Yes. I just got my license a few weeks ago. You wouldn't happen to know anyone who needs a broker to sell something would you?"

"No," Rylee said. "I mean, yes, I do, but…" she paused. She could not work with Bryan. She needed to limit her time with him lest the old feelings come back, and she'd have to make the same decision she did before—to leave not only Cranberry Bay but also Bryan. Rylee lifted her shoulders and looked Bryan in the eyes.

"This isn't anything against your company, which I'm sure is wonderful," she smiled tightly. "But I'd like to use a real estate agent from the Portland area. I think they might know a bigger market of people who would be interested in the home."

"Most of the agents in Portland aren't too interested in our market," Bryan said smoothly, without a trace of disappointment in his voice. "But you might get lucky and find someone who wants to pick something up. Of course," he reached into his pocket and pulled out a card. "If you change your mind, here is my card. Not that you need it," he said and grinned. "Anyone in town can point you in my direction. I'm the only agent in Cranberry Bay."

Rylee stared at his card and then back up to his cheerful face. She shook her head at what she'd always seen as naïve foolishness, believing so firmly that everything was as simple as a mind shift. Rylee held the card tightly in her hand, turned on her heel, and walked toward the bakery. She would never ask Bryan to sell her grandmother's home. She couldn't risk working with him and losing her heart to him again. She needed to obtain as much distance as possible from the man she had once loved. In the morning, she'd call a well-known agency in Portland. She'd tell them there were a few problems, but she was taking care of them. She'd stage the house and take some pictures, without showing any of the problems, of course. The home would be on the market within days, and, hopefully, an offer would be on the table in a few weeks. She'd be on her way to San Diego by Thanksgiving, and Bryan Shuster would go back in her heart to a memory, exactly the place he should be.

Chapter Four

Bryan took a left off the main highway and turned onto a long gravel driveway, as he headed toward a two-story carriage house. Less than a year ago, Sawyer had converted the old barn to a one-bedroom home with a large sleeping loft. It'd been the final piece of his massive fifteen-acre estate, which sat five miles outside of town. Lauren chose the bright-yellow exterior paint, and its cheerful hue and timed matching porch lights welcomed him home on dark, rainy late fall nights like tonight.

Across the expansive yard, lights blazed from every window of Sawyer's sprawling two-story home. Frowning, Bryan parked his truck and headed toward the front of the mansion. Sawyer and Lauren lived in the back of the 3,000-square-foot home, and the front room lights were rarely turned on. His heart dropped into his wet boots as a sudden burst of fear that something might be wrong with Lauren flashed across his mind. It'd only been a couple of hours since he left Sawyer and Adam entertaining Lauren with a board game while Mom knitted a pair of socks in front of the fireplace. But a lot could happen in a couple of hours. Ever since Dad had died of a sudden heart attack, they all knew how fast things could change and never took a moment together for granted.

He hustled down the stone walkway and up the brick stairs. Pumpkins didn't glow on this porch, but Bryan wasn't surprised. Sawyer had stopped celebrating holidays at his home after his wife died. The carriage house and Sawyer's home used the same lock, and Bryan easily inserted his key and pushed open the heavy black front door. His footsteps echoed on the marble-tiled floor. A baby grand piano sat in the corner of the living room. Above it hung a huge, limited edition painting of a sunrise over the Pacific Ocean. Large, white porcelain vases filled with fake flowers sat on a tall sideboard, and a huge wavy-shaped glass bowl perched on a tall entry table. A thick, plush Oriental rug stretched across each end of the living room and another rug ran through the formal dining room underneath a heavy oak table and a matching set of ten chairs. Bryan couldn't remember the last time guests sat at the table for a celebration or ate from the silver and twenty-five china place settings. The entire front of the home reminded him of a museum, and sadness permeated every crevice of his body. Usually, he avoided coming in through the front door, and, instead, entered through the back of the house, which opened into an inviting kitchen where Sawyer and Lauren spent most of their time together.

Hurrying to get out of the living room, Bryan's footsteps echoed on the tiled hallway, and he rounded the corner and stepped into the yellow lit kitchen. Sawyer leaned against a large granite-tiled island in the center of the room. A great living room with a massive stone gas fireplace and large screen TV mounted on the wall opened beyond the kitchen. Pictures of Lauren at various ages from a baby through her current age of ten covered the light green walls, and bookcases filled with framed pictures and books of all genres filled the entire back wall. Heavy rain dripped down the outside of French doors, which opened onto a large patio. In the summer, Sawyer often barbecued and played catch with Lauren in the well-manicured yard.

Now, Lauren lay across a leather sectional couch, tucked alongside a thick pillow. Her maroon backpack lay open on the table. Graded papers and a November school calendar spilled out and onto the thick cream-colored rug. The TV blasted the last game of the World Series.

The smell of freshly brewed coffee filled the room, and a tall woman, wearing blue jeans and dark black sweater, poured steaming coffee into a cup.

"I'm sorry." Bryan stepped backward. "I didn't realize you had company. I thought something might be wrong. All the front lights are on."

"The light timer is broken." Sawyer held a cup of steaming coffee in his hand. "Someone..." he raised an eyebrow and looked in Lauren's direction, "was playing around where she shouldn't have been."

"That's good to hear. I was worried something happened to one of you." Relief washed through Bryan's chest as the woman at the counter set the coffeepot on the burner and turned toward him.

"Hey, little brother." Lisa's hazel eyes, so like his own, greeted him.

"Younger only by two minutes." Bryan stepped forward and wrapped his twin in a large bear hug. He couldn't help but notice how thin she felt in his arms. Dark shadows rimmed her eyes, and her long black sweater and jeans hung on her. "What do we owe this unexpected visit to?"

Lisa picked up the steaming cup of coffee. "I thought a visit to Cranberry Bay for Thanksgiving might be nice." She took a long drink of coffee and swallowed.

Bryan glanced at the calendar Sawyer always kept plastered to the wall. The calendar advertised his construction company, and each page had a plastered yellow logo across the bottom. Halloween was in two days; Thanksgiving wasn't for another three weeks. Either Lisa had her holidays mixed up, or something was going on.

The bathroom door, off the kitchen, opened, and a tall, thin girl stepped out. She adjusted her long, thin black leggings over a black skirt, which looked like it had seen better days. "Where is my room in this huge house? I want to get unpacked." She carried a cell phone in her hand and glanced down at it.

"Maddie." Bryan's eyes widened in surprise at the sight of his niece. The last time he'd seen her, she'd been a thirteen-year-old with bright eyes and a cheerful smile who looked a lot like Lauren. She and Lisa had come for Sawyer's wife's memorial, and Maddie kept them all from crying with her sharp sense of humor and bright wit. Now, at age seventeen, a scowl crossed her thin and narrow face, and he couldn't make out her eyes underneath heavy black eyeliner, mascara, and eye shadow.

"Hey." Maddie grunted in his direction as she crossed the kitchen floor and pulled out one of the stools at the center island. She dropped her cell phone on the counter and dragged her heavy black boots along the metal ring running along the bottom. Mud scraped off her boots and onto the floor.

"I told you to take off your boots," Lisa said, snapping at her daughter.

Maddie glared back at her mother but didn't move to remove her boots.

"Your Mom said take off your boots," Bryan said, trying to support his sister without angering his niece.

Maddie glared at him and slowly leaned down and untied one of her boots. With a loud thump, she let it drop to the kitchen floor. Dirt splayed everywhere beneath her. She did the same with the second boot, and another large pile of mud accumulated on the floor.

Bryan stepped to the kitchen closet, opened the door, and pulled out a broom and a dustpan. He walked to Maddie and handed the items to her.

Maddie ignored the broom and dustpan in Bryan's outstretched hand.

Bryan shook his head and swept the floor under Maddie's feet, scooping up brown dirt into the dustpan.

"It's okay." Sawyer picked up the broom and set it back in the closet. "We'll deal with things later."

"So," Maddie asked, ignoring Bryan and turning to Sawyer. "Where am I sleeping?"

"We need to talk about that." Sawyer padded across the kitchen tile toward the large-screen TV. "I think we just got a run." He clapped his hands together in a fist and raised it in the air. "Might be hope for us in this series after all."

"Daddy!" Lauren protested from the couch. "I can't concentrate on my homework."

"What are you studying?" Lisa stepped over to the couch and sank into the plush cushions beside Lauren. She leaned closer to Lauren.

"Math." Lauren scrunched her nose.

"You don't like math?"

"I like math," Lauren said. "But…"

"She doesn't like Mrs. Williams." Sawyer finished for his daughter.

"She's still teaching?" Lisa swung around and faced Bryan. "She taught our class and that was, what, over twenty years ago."

Bryan shrugged. "It's not easy to find teachers who want to move to Cranberry Bay. If they live out here, they want to teach in the beach schools and live by the coast."

"I hate her." Lauren crumpled her paper, and tears pooled in her eyes. "I'm flunking fourth grade."

"You can't be flunking fourth grade. Math is only one subject. I bet you're doing great in reading and science." Lisa pulled Lauren close to her. "Maybe Maddie would like to work with you. She's good in math, right sweetie?" Lauren turned and smiled a tight smile at her daughter.

"Is it a paying job?" Maddie asked, lifting her eyes away from her obsessive study of her cell phone and up to her Mom.

"Of course not." Lisa snapped. "Lauren is your niece. She's family."

"Oh." Maddie drew a circle with her finger on the island's granite counter. "I was hoping to make some money, for college and everything."

"Family helps each other." Bryan stepped toward Maddie. "We'll deal with college when it gets here."

"Okay, I guess. It looks like I'll have the time here to help her. There's nothing to do in this dump of a town."

Bryan shook his head. He wasn't sure what had happened to Maddie in the time since he'd seen her last, but she was not the same sweet girl he remembered. He reached into the cabinet above his head and pulled down a heavy blue coffee cup. Maddie was still a child. She may be a surly one, but she was still a child. Inside all of that rudeness, she was still the niece he loved, and he was determined to win her affections again.

He poured himself a cup of coffee, dumped a spoonful of sugar into the black liquid, and reached into the cabinet above his head to pull down a bag of chocolate cream cookies that Sawyer always kept on hand. The bag was unopened, and Bryan carried it to the island, ripped off the top, and pulled out a seat beside Maddie. "Cookie?" He held out the bag.

Maddie shook her head. She moved her cell phone away from Bryan and stuck it into her jacket pocket.

Bryan pulled out two sandwich cookies. "How are you?" He eased back on the stool. He was used to working with teens. He had a regular rotation of kids during the summer parks season. Sometimes there was someone who didn't want to work the job. Usually, with a little patience and kindness, the teen would come around.

"I hate this place." Maddie slumped onto her stool. She placed her head between her hands.

"This place?" Bryan twisted one of the cookies open and placed the chocolate cookie top on the counter. "I kinda thought Sawyer's house was a pretty cool place to be myself. There's this great kitchen. He's always got good cookies." Bryan raised one of the chocolate cookies to Maddie in a toast.

"Not here," Maddie raised her voice. "I hate Cranberry Bay."

"That's enough!" Lisa said sharply and stood up. She ran her hands through her hair. "We talked about this and agreed there would be no negative talk about Cranberry Bay."

Bryan unscrewed the second cookie top and placed it beside the first. He merged the two cookies together to make one cookie with extra icing. "How long are you staying?" he asked his niece.

"Too long." Maddie turned away from him and stared at the table.

Bryan raised an eyebrow at his sister.

"For awhile," she said. "We need to get out of Seattle for a little bit. There was some trouble with Maddie." Lisa's lips tightened.

"Just say it, Mom," Maddie said. "I stole a few things and had to spend some time at the juvenile detention center. I'm a criminal."

Lisa crossed her hands over her chest. "You are not a criminal. You just got in with some wrong people."

Maddie shrugged and turned toward the TV.

"We'll get through this," Bryan said, reassuring his sister. Family was important, and they had always supported each other. "You'll be staying with Sawyer? He's got a lot of great rooms upstairs."

Sawyer cleared his throat and stepped away from the TV. "I'm giving them the carriage house."

"The carriage house? I thought that was the place I rented." Bryan pushed back the stool and stood up. The carriage house had one bedroom and a loft. It wasn't big enough for the three of them.

"Sorry, brother." Sawyer lowered his voice. "I know it's going to break the lease I set up with you. But I thought you might want to move into Mom's house for awhile. She needs a little extra hand around the place. You'd be closer to your office."

"Mom's house?" Bryan paced the kitchen. If he had a job, he could have bought his own place and then none of this would have mattered. But he had only just gotten his real estate license. He'd inherited some listings from the retired agent, Rob Decker, but he hadn't gotten a bite yet.

Sawyer cleared his throat. "Mom took a small fall the other day. She banged up her ankle pretty good. She insisted she was fine, but I don't think it's so great for her to be living alone."

"Mom fell?" Bryan's heart leapt in his chest. "Why didn't she say something?"

"You know Mom," Sawyer said, and smiled lightly at his brother. "She's not going to admit she needs help."

Bryan nodded and bit his lower lip. Mom wouldn't admit to anyone she needed help. If she fell, she'd never tell her boys for fear of worrying them. Even though all of them were grown men, more than capable and willing to protect and care for her, Mom still thought of them as her little boys, people she needed to protect.

"She could move in here." Lisa grabbed a cookie. "There are plenty of rooms," she muttered as crumbs fell out of her mouth. Lisa absently swiped the crumbs off her sweater. Guiltily, she peeked at Sawyer. "Sorry. I'll pick it up."

Bryan smiled. Neatness had never been his twin's strength. As children, her room always won the messiest-room competition. She spent hours on Saturday mornings trying to clean it up.

"Mom will never move out," Bryan said firmly. His mother would never leave the home where she'd raised her family and lived with their Dad. Lisa didn't understand the connection a person could have with a place or a home, not after moving to Seattle where she and Maddie had lived in half-a-dozen apartments.

"You're right," Lisa said. "Mom is not going to want to accept help if she knows we're trying to keep an eye on her. But maybe she will understand if you move in because of Maddie and me taking over the carriage house."

Bryan rubbed his forehead. Mom would love to have Lisa and Maddie in Cranberry Bay. But how would she feel about him living in his old bedroom? She often said how much she enjoyed her own space after years of raising a large family. How would he feel about being back in his bedroom? The same bedroom where he'd once spent nights dreaming of Rylee Harper.

"Rylee Harper's grandmother's home is just a few streets over from Mom's house." Sawyer leaned back against the counter and crossed his arms over his chest.

"Yes." Bryan eyed his brother.

"What does Rylee Harper have to do with this?" Lisa asked and frowned.

"Nothing," Bryan said, not wanting to explain to his twin about the bet. He turned to Sawyer. "I'll move in with Mom."

"Thanks, brother." Lisa hopped over the stool and put her arm around him. Maddie slid off her stool and sulked to the couch, where she crashed in a heap, as far away from Lauren as possible. Lauren scrunched up her eyes like she might cry. But before the tears started, a hardened look that seemed a lot like Maddie's crossed her face.

Bryan frowned. The last thing he wanted was Maddie's bad attitude rubbing off on Lauren. As soon as possible, he was going to pull his older niece aside and talk to her. He wanted Maddie to know she was a part of this family, no matter what.

Chapter Five

The furnace hummed as Rylee dunked her peppermint tea bag in hot water. Raisin lay in front of the brightly burning gas fireplace. Occasionally, he raised his head to eye the tall, heavyset man who stood on a ladder beneath the hole in the plaster ceiling. Rylee carried her tea into the living room and nodded in satisfaction at the glowing table lamps, the dusted coffee table, and the freshly washed curtains. In the last three days, she'd been able to make a good deal of progress on the home. The utilities were all in her name. The gutters were clean. She'd even found an old mower in the garage and trimmed the front and backyards on a cold, but sunny afternoon. Once the ceiling plaster was fixed, she'd get the home on the market.

The only problem was getting someone to look at the leak in the ceiling. She'd placed calls to four different plumbers, and it'd taken over two days for anyone to return her call and schedule a time to come out to look at the house. This morning, when Jim arrived, he took one look at the plaster and shook his head; for the last two hours, he had been scouting around the house, checking the pipes in the two upstairs bathrooms, the kitchen, and under the home.

Jim stepped down from the ladder and jotted a few more notes on what looked like a full yellow tablet.

"How does it look?" Rylee smiled brightly.

"Not good." He shook his head. "You've got a serious water leak, and these can be complicated."

"How much is it going to cost?" Rylee set her teacup down on a colorful fabric coaster. She'd made the coasters with a small plastic loom. The loom was probably still tucked away in a box in the attic; it was one of the places she hadn't been able to face yet.

"I'm still working out the cost," Jim said, looking at the paper and frowning. "But I think we're easily into a couple thousand dollars."

"A couple thousand dollars." Rylee gasped, running her hand through her hair.

"Sorry for the bad news. But water leaks in the plaster don't just come from where they are dripping. In your case, it's actually coming from the roof, but the water ran down the upstairs floorboards before it pooled in the corner over there and caused the plaster damage that you see."

"The roof needs to be repaired too?" Rylee could barely find her voice.

"It looks like it." Jim said. "At least on the left-hand side of the home."

"How soon can someone start work on all of this? I'm hoping to get it on the market as soon as possible."

Jim frowned. "I've got a couple great guys who can do the work, but they're pretty backed up right now. The new beach grocery superstore is trying to open for the holidays, and the guys are working twenty-four seven. It'll be at least early December before I can get anyone over here."

"You're telling me the work can't even start until after Thanksgiving?"

"We can patch things up for you," Jim said. "We want to get the roof fixed first, so you don't have any more leaks. But the bulk of the interior work, tearing out the ceiling and taking care of the damage, yes, that will all have to wait until the first week of December."

"I see," Rylee said, trying to keep herself calm and her nerves steady. "And how long will everything take?"

Jim looked up to the ceiling. "As long as we don't have any big storms that cause roof damage to people's homes and pull the guys off the job here, I'd say we're looking at about a two- to three-week time frame."

"Two to three weeks." Rylee mentally ran through the dates. "The work won't be finished until just before Christmas."

"That's right, but," Jim said, and smiled at her, "that'll be perfect because people aren't really looking to buy a house in the holiday season. You can get a good jump on the spring listings in January."

"Yes," Rylee muttered. "Perfect." She had wanted to be out of Cranberry Bay by the end of the month; now it looked like she wouldn't be able to even get the house on the market for two months. Her savings account would never stretch, let alone cover the repairs. She'd have to find a job and, most likely, take out a small home-equity loan to cover the repairs.

"Do you need some time to think about it?"

"No." Rylee shook her head. The last thing she wanted was more delays. "Let's go ahead and schedule. If you can take care of the roof now, I'll wait until after Thanksgiving for the rest of the work."

"Sure thing," Jim said. "I'll get the guys over here tomorrow morning, and we'll get everything squared away for you." He slipped the yellow tablet into his black bag and grabbed a thick black coat from the hall tree. "Nice place you have here. Too bad you're selling. It looks like someone loved this house very much."

"Yes," Rylee said as an unexpected bubble of tears gathered in her throat. Her Grandparents weren't the only ones who had loved this house. Cranberry Bay was her place of warmth, comfort, and family. But all that had changed. Now, with her Grandparents gone, she just wanted to sell the house and start over in a city where she could be anonymous, the way it had always been with her family.

"We'll see you in the morning, bright and early." Jim pulled open the door, and a gust of wind brought leaves dancing into the hallway.

With her left foot, Rylee pushed the leaves back onto the porch and shut the door behind Jim. She leaned against the wood and rubbed her eyes. Where would she find a job in Cranberry Bay? From the looks of what she'd seen so far, there wasn't much in town for someone with a background in design or even a small job working as a clerk in a bustling shop. She stepped away from the door and walked to the end of the living room. Opening a small door, Rylee walked into her grandmother's sewing room. White built-in shelves lined the walls. Colorful fabric was stacked neatly on the shelves. An old Singer sewing machine covered with a paisley cloth sat on a wooden table. A set of pillowcases was tucked into a large basket on the floor. Rylee picked up one of the pillowcases and ran her hands over the pale pink fabric. For as long as she could remember, Grandma always had a booth at the annual Cranberry Bay Holiday Craft Fair. Held in a small church, the fair was filled with local residents who hoped to buy a handcrafted item. As a child, she spent summers helping Grandma create small cloth-ornament dolls or green-and-red tree-skirts with festive sparkles.

A white flyer tossed haphazardly in the side of the basket caught Rylee's eye. She reached in and read about a spring fabric sale at the New Leaf Sewing Shop. Had Grandma gone to the sale, or did she only hope to get there? Rylee noted the address as Main Street. It wouldn't hurt to stop in and see if they knew of anyone who needed design work. Maybe there was no one in Cranberry Bay who wanted a commercial designer, but perhaps one of the hotels at the beach needed a redo of a few of their rooms or a front entry. She didn't need a huge job, just something to tide her over for the next two months and pay for repairs.

Rylee stepped out of the room to find Raisin waiting at the door, his tail banging against the wall. She glanced outside. The wind still blew at a good clip, but the sun had come out.

"Come on, boy," Rylee said, picking up his leather leash. "Let's go for a walk."

Fifteen minutes later, Rylee stood in front of the New Leaf Sewing Shop. The lights shone brightly, but she couldn't see anyone working at the front counter. Pulling the door open, Rylee turned to Raisin and lifted her hand to her lips as if the dog would understand her. "Shh...don't bark."

A burst of laughter came from the back of the store. Four women were gathered around a long table with an assortment of pattern pieces and colorful fabric.

"I'm sorry." Rylee stepped backward and pulled on Raisin's leash. "I didn't realize this was a private class." Raisin didn't budge. He wagged his tail and let out a sharp bark, as if to say hello. Mortified, Rylee jerked his leash and pulled him toward the door.

A tall, slender woman stepped out from behind the table. She wore a long, colorful brown-and-tan striped knit skirt and a matching cream sweater. "Welcome to New Leaf. I'm Katie Coos, the owner. Excuse me for not greeting you when you came in. The apron club is a little excited about our project this week," She smiled brightly at Rylee. "How can I help you?"

Katie Coos. The name was instantly familiar to Rylee. "You probably don't remember me. But I used to visit my Grandma. We stopped by the scrapbook and paper shop at least once a week, sometimes more if I could convince Grandma." She laughed to herself. "I had so many craft and business ideas. I think Grandma was always glad to see me leave at the end of the summer, so she could rest."

"Rylee Harper!" Katie said, and smiled. "Mom wanted me to be just like you, and I didn't want anything to do with the scrapbook shop. I only wanted to play softball and swim in the river."

"And now you own this place."

"Yes." Katie's face darkened, and her eyes dropped to the floor. "Mom got sick and couldn't keep up. I took the store over, but," she shrugged, "scrapbooking never was my thing. I've always loved fabrics and textiles, and once I figured out how to sew, well…" Katie looked up, her eyes shining bright. "Here we are."

"And she has one of the best shops in the northern part of Oregon. People come from all over to purchase her fabric and special order." A dark-haired woman spoke as she cut into fabric, carefully following a pinned pattern.

Katie shook her head, but a smile tucked into her lips. "Friends. What would we do without them?"

Rylee's chest ached as she thought of her best friend. She believed Ericka would have stood up for her no matter what, but that hadn't happened.

"I'm looking for work." Rylee pushed the sharply painful memories away. She cleared her throat. Her palms felt damp, and she resisted wiping them on her jeans. She gave Raisin's leash a tight little tug. He looked up and leaned into her left leg, sensing she needed comfort. As a top designer in Vegas, she'd grown accustomed to not looking for work. Now, she felt awkward and uncomfortable, but she didn't have any choice. Rylee squared her shoulders and faced Katie. "I wondered if you knew of anyone who might want a designer."

"No. I'm sorry." Katie turned to the women gathered around the table behind her. "Ivy? Gracie? Sasha? Do you know of anyone looking for a designer?"

"I wish," Gracie said. "The River Rock Inn could use a new look in the rooms. But," she shrugged, "it's not exactly like business is booming in Cranberry Bay."

"I would love help at the bakery, too." Sasha's piercing dark eyes darted to Rylee and then back to Katie. "But I can't afford to hire anyone. Tiffany comes in on weekends, and I rope Tyler into helping me package up some of the mass orders for the sports team celebrations." She smiled at Raisin. "But I do have one ten-year-old boy who would love to walk your dog if you need someone."

"Thank you." Rylee took a step backward and tugged on Raisin's leash. "I'll remember the offer."

"I'm afraid I don't need help either," Ivy said from the left-hand corner of the table. "The antique shop isn't exactly booming these days. Old items from attics and garages barely cover the bills. I'm sorry."

"Thank you." Rylee fiddled with Raisin's leash. "I'm sorry to have interrupted your sewing club." Don't give up, she told herself. This was just the first stop. She didn't expect to find a job immediately. In the morning, she'd drive over to some of the towns along the coast and look for design work in the beach hotels.

"Wait." Katie said. "If you'd like to sew, we'd love for you to join the sewing club. We're just beginning this month's apron pattern."

"I do sew," Rylee said, thinking of the bolts of unused fabric sitting in her grandmother's sewing room and the sewing machine. "But…" Her mind raced for an excuse. She wasn't in Cranberry Bay to make connections. She planned to take care of business and leave.

Before she could find the words, the bell on the shop tinkled and a woman called out, "Hello. Katie? Sasha?"

"Lisa!" In a smattering of excited voices and hugs, the four women rushed forward and engulfed the tall, thin woman at the door. As the group's voices rose in chatter, Rylee stared past the woman to Bryan standing behind her. He smiled broadly at her.

"I was hoping I might find you here," Bryan said, stepping around Lisa and into the shop. "I thought I might ask a favor."

"Yes?" Rylee tried to control her beating heart, which sped up every time she saw Bryan. The tone of his voice reminded her of how well he could charm her. She vowed not to let it happen this time.

"Well," Bryan said, smiling his boyish grin at her. "I hope this isn't too forward. But your grandfather had a lot of great car tools. My brother collects vintage cars. I'd like to stop by and take a look at your grandfather's tool collection. That is, if you didn't have something else you were doing with it."

Rylee took a step backward as Bryan stepped closer to her. "I don't have anything else I'm doing with it. I didn't really know the collection was still in the garage." She swallowed hard. She wanted so badly to lean against him and feel his arms around her. She wanted to press her cheek against his scratchy shirt and hear the beating of his heart. In his arms, she always felt safe and protected.

"I could stop by one day this week?"

"Yes." A memory flashed across her mind of Bryan working with her grandfather in the garage, wearing his cut-off shorts and tank top. She flushed thinking of how she'd been so enamored with him in those teenage summer days. Who was she kidding? She was still affected by him. The only difference was she wasn't a teenage girl, and she could control her emotions. She hoped.

"Rylee." Katie spoke above the chatter of women. "You will join us, won't you? The sewing circle meets on Wednesday nights. We're sewing a pleated Thanksgiving apron."

"Yes." Rylee said, seeing a way out of spending more time with Bryan. "I would love to come Wednesday nights." She turned to Bryan, "Why don't you stop by on Wednesday evening; I'll leave the garage door open for you." She took a deep breath. Bryan did not have to rule her every thought and feeling. She was no longer a teenager falling all over her first love. She was a grown woman who knew how to handle life on life's terms.

"Sure thing." Bryan nodded to her. His face was void of any emotion except politeness. Rylee's stomach turned with sadness. She didn't want to fall in love with Bryan again, but she did want to know she had once mattered. Of course, he'd been married. He'd fallen in love with someone else. Although he was no longer married, she couldn't expect him to remain in love with her forever. But she still wanted to see something in his eyes. Something to tell her she had once mattered to him the way he had to her.

Bryan turned away and sauntered over to the sewing circle women. "So, who is going to make me an apron?"

Giggles and laughter rose from the five women clustered together, and Rylee couldn't help but notice how Sasha's arm went around Bryan's waist in a light hug as she gazed up at him. Not wanting to see any more, Rylee pulled on Raisin's leash and slipped out the door. The cool rainy breeze blew across her cheeks, and she took a deep breath. She simply needed to put Bryan back in his place as someone she once knew and get on with her plan to get out of Cranberry Bay.

Chapter Six

Bryan frowned at the photos on his computer screen. He took a sip of cold coffee and swallowed. The late afternoon shadows crept into the small room, and he flicked on the seashell desk lamp. It'd been in the throwaway pile at Ivy's antique shop. Ivy said the shop already had five seashell lamps, and they didn't need one more. She handed it to him for free, and he set it up on his desk as his first piece of office furnishing. The large conch shell reminded him of a trip he'd taken with his brothers and Dad to Hawaii. It had been one of the only trips they'd taken where Bryan could remember his Dad enjoying himself.

Restlessly, Bryan shifted on the hard swivel chair. For the last hour, he'd tried to come up with catchy captions that would encourage buyers to request a showing. Former agent Rob Decker hadn't believed in using technology to promote his business. He'd been in business long enough that he had a long list of satisfied clients who, in turn, gave him a steady stream of new clients. As a new agent, Bryan needed the online Multiple Listing Service to attract buyers. He only wished writing one-liners about a home's marvelous backyard with a play-area for kids didn't have him staring at the screen for over an hour.

A gust of cool wind blew inside the small office as the door opened, and a burly man entered the room. He wore a thick, heavy black down coat, jeans, and tall leather boots. Bryan pushed back his chair and squeezed between the large maple desk and the wall. He stepped forward and embraced the man in a large bear hug. "Dennis. How have you been?"

"Good." Dennis returned the hug. "Got a minute?'

"Always." Bryan gathered a stack of manila folders from a chair and placed the files on the floor. "Sorry about the mess. I'm trying to update some of Rob's listings."

"Allison and I heard you took over for Rob. How are things going?"

"Slow. But it's the time of year. How is Mrs. Perkins?" Bryan asked, and smiled at the thought of his first-grade teacher. Allison Perkins was a longtime resident of Cranberry Bay whom everyone still called Mrs. Perkins. She'd retired last year after a thirty-five-year teaching career. The town held a large celebration for her in the park. Her former students had returned from all over the country, and the day had included a marvelous afternoon of stories, tears, and joy.

"She's getting used to retirement." Dennis ran his hand over his lower jaw. "But, we've decided to sell the river fishing cottages. Our grandkids are in California, and we'd like to buy a condo closer to them."

A memory of the old fishing cottages flashed across Bryan's mind. On the night Rylee turned twenty-one, they had slipped into one of the cottages with a key he'd found tucked under a flower mat. The rustic cottages offered very little comfort, but that hadn't mattered to them. He'd brought a thick blanket, and they'd placed it in front of the stone fireplace, talking all night and dreaming of a future together. He had proposed not soon after. Foolishly, he believed that night would lead to her spending the rest of her life with him. Their lives seemed wide-open and filled with promise.

"Do you think you can help us with the sale?" Dennis repeated.

Bryan flushed and cleared his throat, embarrassed to be caught lost in his daydreams and not paying attention to business. "I'd be happy to help you with the sale of the cottages. These are the six cottages alongside the west bank of the river, correct?"

Dennis shifted in his chair, leaned forward, and tapped his fingers on the desk. "Yes. Those are the ones. I've used a couple for storing fishing gear and other items from our house." Dennis shook his head. "I'm afraid one of the cottages is loaded up with nothing but Christmas boxes. I'll ask Allison to clear it out as soon as possible."

Bryan chuckled. "Mom would love a spare cottage to store Christmas decorations. She must have saved every snowflake and Santa picture my brothers and sister and I ever made. Mom keeps saying one day she'll have a house full of grandkids to enjoy the old things. So far, there's only two, and it doesn't look like any more are on the way." He ran his finger over the edge of a manila folder on his desk. His chest ached with the unfilled longing for children, his children, running around his home.

"You never know how things will work out," Dennis said. "Mrs. Perkins and I didn't have our kids until late in life. There's plenty of time left."

"Yes, well..." Bryan reached into his desk and pulled out a thick sheaf of papers. Before he could even think about a family, he needed to focus on making an income. "Let me get some information from you. I'll have the cottages up on the multiple listings by this evening and add a few photos tomorrow."

Dennis cleared his throat. "Allison thinks the cottages would sell better if they were fixed up a bit. I told her fishing cottages were always popular. But she seemed to think otherwise."

"Houses do sell better if they are staged." Bryan twirled his pen between his fingers. "The market isn't exactly booming in Cranberry Bay and staging them to be vacation cottages would help the sale. They're sold as a single listing, yes?"

"Yes. All six cottages are one lot."

"Is the staging something Mrs. Perkins wants to do?"

"No." Dennis lowered his voice as a shadow crossed his face. "I'm afraid not. She doesn't want this to get around town, so please don't say anything." Dennis swallowed. "She's been sick lately. The doctors aren't sure what's wrong. We've taken a lot of trips to see doctors in Portland, and they're doing some tests."

Bryan's heart contracted. He adored his teacher. As a first-grader, he was slow to catch on to reading. Instead of allowing him to slip behind, Mrs. Perkins spent long afternoons teaching him how to sound out letters. By the end of the year, he had advanced into second grade as a reader.

"I'm so sorry to hear. I'll take care of the staging. We'll work it on a commission basis and take the payment from the sale of the cottages."

"Thank you." Dennis nodded to him and stood. "I know your Dad would be proud of you."

Bryan lowered his eyes and fiddled with his pen. He doubted his Dad would be proud of him. He'd become exactly what Dad had always suspected he would—someone who didn't have a direction or a strong focus but instead floated from low-paying job to low-paying job.

"Of course he'd be proud," Dennis said, his voice echoing off the empty office walls. "Your Dad always talked about how proud he was of all of you."

"Of course," Bryan said. He clenched his jaw and bit back the shame he'd known all his life. Dad hadn't been proud of him. Unlike his brothers and sister, he'd been a disappointment to his father. He didn't excel at baseball like Sawyer. He didn't excel at basketball like Adam. He didn't like sports at all. Instead, all he wanted to do was play his guitar. His father lectured him on how music would never get him anywhere besides a tavern at the beach. And, Bryan's chest tightened, his father had been right. He'd tried to make a living as a musician and quickly discovered playing nightly gigs at the beach taverns wouldn't cover the rent. Seasonal work never paid enough, and most people had to juggle multiple jobs in order to live full time in the small beach communities surrounding Cranberry Bay.

Bryan pushed the painful memories aside. He stood and leaned over the desk to shake Dennis's hand. "We'll be in touch soon. Please tell Mrs. Perkins I said hello."

After Dennis left, the silence in the small office chilled him. He'd never worked well by himself, preferring instead to be surrounded by life and activity. Bryan grabbed his black leather over-the-shoulder bag and shoved a couple of folders inside. He slipped his small laptop computer into the largest compartment of the bag and pulled his jacket from a small nail behind the door. Outside, the air smelled of fires crackling in wood-burning stoves. Bryan made a mental note to make sure Mom had enough dry wood to last for the next couple months. He headed down the hill toward the local pub.

A minute later, he pulled open the heavy wooden door. A fire crackled in the stone fireplace, and a large-screen TV broadcast a college football game on the corner wall. Tom Hathaway, owner of the town hardware store, played a game of pool with Chuck Dawson, owner of the tackle-and-boat-rental shop.

"Want to join us?" Chuck lowered his cue to the table. He leaned down and cued the ball into the right pocket.

"No, thanks." Bryan patted his black satchel. "I've got a little work to do."

Bryan strode by the bar, where Josh Morton and Jack Richardson studied a long spreadsheet. Josh ran the town's historic train from the small depot. Once the town had been on the way to Portland, but all that changed a few years ago when the train companies realized the tourists didn't want to come to Cranberry Bay. They wanted to go to the beach towns. Josh's grandfather had spent his career as a train conductor, and, after he passed away, Josh had set up a nonprofit for the town's old train depot and surrounding tracks. On fall weekends, Josh ran a special fall-leaves train ride that always brought a flurry of people to Cranberry Bay. But the signature event was the Santa train, complete with hot cocoa and cookies and children wearing their pajamas. The event was a favorite of Lauren's, and she always convinced all of them to make it a family occasion. Unfortunately, most of the time heavy winds and rainstorms pounded the area, and the holiday train drew only small groups of locals.

Bryan headed toward the back corner booth and quickly sank onto the hard bench. As he waited for his laptop to boot up, he ran his fingers over etched initials carved in the tabletop. It'd been a ritual for Cranberry Bay couples to carve their names in the tables. His parents' initials were on the table under the front window. Sawyer and Ginger had carved theirs in a front table by the door. And, if he walked to the table in the far right-hand corner, he'd find Rylee's and his initials, etched together and encircled with a heart. They'd worked on it for weeks the summer they both turned twenty-one. After she left, he never sat at their table.

Bryan's computer beeped as Ivy stepped alongside his table. A brown-and-cream apron covered her jeans and maroon sweater. "What can I get you?"

"I didn't know you were working at the pub?" Bryan raised his eyebrows. Ivy's antique business was one of the few in the town that visitors stopped for on their way to Seashore Cove. Over the last few years, she'd built a strong track record of online sales and kept busy year-round. Unlike other locals, she didn't need to juggle multiple jobs.

"Caitlin's got a nasty flu. Jessica is visiting her sister in college. Bill said we wouldn't be busy tonight. I told him I'd fill in for a few hours. If I can sell antiques, I can sell a few pints of beer." Ivy's light laughter filled the space between them.

"I'm a part of the microbrew club." Bryan reached into his wallet for the small, folded card. Every month, he collected a new stamp. At the end of the year, the cards were tossed into a drawing for a free month of drinks. He'd won the first year, but he had quietly slipped his card to Chuck, who'd just lost his son in a car wreck on an icy road.

"Ah." Ivy leaned back on her heels. "You're one of the lucky. I'll check with Bill to see about the flavor of the month. I'm guessing Pumpkin Ale."

"That was last month." Bryan laid his card on the table and smoothed it with his thumb. "It's November. New month. New beer."

"Gotcha, sir," Ivy said, playfully. "Do I take the card too?"

"Yep." Bryan pushed it toward her. He smiled at her. Ivy and his twin sister had been best friends all through school. She'd joined them at family holidays and always brought a lot of laughter. No one could understand why Ivy hadn't found that special partner, but Bryan suspected it had something to do with her feelings for Josh. Something that Josh seemed not to notice. "Bill has a stamp he keeps in the left corner of the bar."

Ivy shook her head. "You ought to be waiting tables, not me."

Bryan shook his head and smiled, as, across the room, Josh waved at Ivy.

She leaned over and whispered against Bryan's cheek. "I'll be right back. Someone is calling me." Ivy lightly stepped through the center of the pub and stopped in front of Josh. She leaned close to him and touched his arm.

Bryan turned back to his work as a song's lyrics blasting from the pub's speakers caught him off-guard. It was the song he had once declared as his and Rylee's. That night, he had pulled his car up alongside the river's bank, opened the door, and let the music seep into the night air. He held her close and danced with her under a full moon. Something inside him ached. The ache that never quite went away, no matter how much he had tried to get rid of it. He shook himself. He couldn't think about any of that now. Those days were gone, and he'd never again trust her with his heart. Bryan pulled the listing data back up on his computer. The best thing to do was focus on his work.

After a few minutes, Ivy set a dark bottle of ale in front of him. "November's special is a handcrafted beer out of Portland JR's Brewing. I can't tell you if it's any good or not. Josh wouldn't give anything away." She laid the folded and stamped card beside him. "But I did get you a stamp for November."

"Thanks." Bryan took a drink. It was a little sweeter than he liked his ale, but he'd never been one to complain.

The front door opened, and a blast of cold air shot through the pub. Councilman Cole Mays and Mayor Mitch Webb stepped inside. Both of them shook their dark jackets, and water splashed off their shoulders. Bryan peered at one of the large upper windows. The trees swayed, and water ran down the outside pane.

Mitch spotted Bryan, nodded, and headed his way. Cole stopped to talk to Jack and Josh.

"You're not trying to work are you?" Mitch slid into the booth opposite him.

"Nah." Bryan shut his manila folder. He grinned at his longtime childhood friend.

"Good. Because the town council meeting is over, and I need a beer." He glanced at the heated game of pool between Chuck and Tom. "Maybe even a good game of pool."

"Bad?" Bryan drank another swig of beer. He wiped his upper lip with his index finger.

"It's always the same." Mitch shook his head. "Until we get some new blood into town with new ideas, nothing is going to change on the council."

"What about some old blood with new ideas?"

"Sounds good," Mitch said. "Someone you know got something? Sawyer?"

Bryan clenched his jaw. Of course, Mitch would assume Sawyer had ideas for how to help Cranberry Bay. Everyone always looked to Sawyer. First captain of the high school baseball team and later as one of the area's largest residential developers.

Cole slipped into the seat beside Mitch. He leaned back and stuck his long legs out from under the table. "What's going on with Sawyer? Did he score some more land?" Cole ran his hand through his thick dark hair.

"Most likely." Bryan took a long swig of his drink. His brother scooped up land like it was a handful of chocolates at a holiday party.

"Got room for one more?" Josh slipped into the booth beside Bryan, jarring him and shoving him to the left corner.

Bryan straightened and gave Josh a playful shove back. "Always." Sometimes he felt closer to his longtime childhood playmates than he did to his own brothers. They'd bonded over an elementary lunchroom table, four apples, and three ice cream sandwiches and had seen each other through the ups and downs of their lives.

"What've you got?" Mitch rubbed his brow. "I'm up for anything at this point. We're really scraping the bottom of the barrel. The elementary school is going to close soon if we can't get some new families in this town. But we need jobs to attract people. Something we're a little short on."

"Well," Bryan's heart pounded in his chest. He hadn't told anyone of his idea. He had wanted to wait until he secured funding before talking about it. But he'd never dream of holding out on his friends. "I think what this town needs is some new fun. We need ways to draw people away from the beach towns and over here for a night or two on their vacations."

"I agree." Mitch said. Ivy set a glass of dark ale on the table, and he took a swig. "We need something for all ages. Fishing and clamming is great, but it doesn't exactly draw the ladies in. We need something that draws them to Cranberry Bay to stay for at least a night."

"Exactly," Bryan said. He cleared his throat. "I've got my eye on a set of riverboats. One is a restaurant, and the other is a casino. It'd be just the thing to encourage people to visit."

"But we're not on tribal lands," Josh said, frowning. "I didn't think gambling could be on land that wasn't tribal."

"Some types of gambling are okay. The state calls it social gambling." Bryan leaned back in the booth. "I've done some research. We can have gambling boats outside of tribal lands. People gamble and win money, but the house can't take a cut of what people make on their winnings."

"But how does the gambling make money for the town?" Mitch said, frowning again. "The riverboats won't do us any good if they're not making money."

"There is a charge for the entrance to the riverboat. We also charge for food and drink, and we offer things like Ladies Nights Out and Poker Nights, where the alcohol flows. All of which require a small cover charge." Bryan straightened and leaned forward. "The best part is the food and drinks require a chef and kitchen staff, as well as waitresses and hostesses. Everything adds up to jobs for Cranberry Bay. People will need somewhere to spend the night afterward. This increases the need for lodging and other businesses along the Main Street. Some of those buildings have been empty for years."

"What kind of gambling games do people play on the boat?" Cole said, eyeing him with interest.

"The basics. Roulette. Craps. Blackjack."

"Sounds great to me," Josh said. "Attracting new people to town would help with the train, too. We could offer more runs if people wanted them." He lowered his voice. "We've got a big repair coming up on one of the engines. We'll have to do a fund-raiser for it."

"Fund-raisers." Mitch snapped his fingers "I bet we could host a lot of fund-raisers on the riverboats."

"Fund-raisers are great," Bryan said. "But the prizes need to be non-cash, which shouldn't be a problem. Everyone loves those baskets loaded with goodies for things like Italian dinners and family game nights." He had won a big chocolate basket during the volunteer firefighters' annual dinner. A lot of the chocolate had landed in Lauren's holiday stocking that year.

"A fancy dinner would be something people could get behind," Mitch said. "My wife was just saying she wished there were more opportunities to get dressed up." He smiled. "I can't say I blame her. I kinda like it myself."

Bryan grinned at Mitch. He'd married his high school sweetheart, and the two of them had been on their honeymoon ever since. They'd been the envy of all their friends, none of whom had found the right partner yet. "So, you think it's a good idea?" A flicker of hope rose in Bryan's chest. "I'll need to propose it to the council and get their approval. It would help if I had you on board first."

"You've got my vote." Cole nodded. "I think it's a great idea. Wish I thought of it myself to tell you the truth."

"You've got my vote," Mitch said. "And I can talk to some of the others and give them a heads-up. But the council will want to know you've secured funding. No one wants another replay of what happened last time."

"I promise it won't be a repeat of last time." Bryan remembered how he'd gotten caught up in the plans for an amusement park with an investor. He'd met the man on a ski trip to Mount Baker, and, after a couple nights in the ski lodge bar, the man had pledged his support for the multimillion-dollar idea. The idea quickly fell apart after the investor saw the statistics on Cranberry Bay, and he backed out of the whole deal at the last second, just before Bryan had been scheduled to take it to a council vote. "Sawyer and I have a deal for some investment monies on this project."

Mitch leaned closer. "Spill it. What's the deal?"

"There's a little bet on the table." Bryan averted his eyes from his friends.

"What's the bet?" Cole leaned forward.

Bryan cleared his throat. "If I can convince Rylee Harper to move to Cranberry Bay, Sawyer will fund the boats."

"Rylee Harper?" Mitch said. "You planned to marry her about ten years ago, right?"

"Yea." Bryan shifted away from his friends and gazed toward the blazing fire in the fireplace. "She's selling her grandmother's home and staying in Cranberry Bay for a few weeks."

"Ah," Mitch said, and shook his head. "The riverboats were a good idea. But, that bet, I don't know…"

"Thanks for the vote of confidence." Bryan punched Mitch in the arm.

"I don't mean to dampen this flame," Cole said. "But what's going to make Rylee move to Cranberry Bay? Didn't she go running out of here last time? And you were practically engaged, right? So, how come it's going to be different?"

"She needs a job," Josh said. He took a long drink of his beer. "I heard she was wandering all over town looking for work the other day. She stopped by the train depot and asked if we needed any help."

"She needs work?" Bryan quickly turned to face Josh. If Rylee needed work, that was a good sign. If she had a job she liked, that was the first step toward convincing her Cranberry Bay could be home.

"Something about repairs on her grandmother's house costing too much and taking longer." Josh shrugged. "Don't tell her you heard it from me."

The river cottages and his conversation with Dennis flashed across Bryan's mind. Excitement pooled in his stomach. It was perfect. Rylee had a background in design. But he doubted the beach towns had looked twice at her. The small towns thrived on using locals, not someone who breezed in from Vegas for a few weeks. The cottage staging would fit what she was looking for to help pay for her grandmother's repairs. And once word got out about her abilities, he suspected the beach hotels would be more interested in her and offer her more work, something she might not be able to refuse. That would ensure him a chance for her to see if Cranberry Bay could be home.

"Excuse me, boys." Bryan slipped his computer and notes into his bag and pushed his unfinished beer toward Josh. "You'll have to finish this for me."

"Where are you going?" Cole asked. "We just got here."

"I've got a job to offer someone," Bryan said. "And," he winked at Mitch. "a bet to win."

Chapter Seven

Rylee wiped her gloved hand over the park bench and brushed away a handful of wet pine needles. She sank down as Raisin plopped by her feet. He tucked his tail around him and leaned his head on her scuffed rain boot. She'd picked up the boots along with a couple of heavy flannel shirts, a thick down jacket, and a pair of jeans at the Goodwill outlet just north of Cranberry Bay. Rylee shivered and wrapped her coat tighter around her.

She stared into the rushing river running below the park and tried to push away the headache forming between her eyes. In the last week, she'd been everywhere looking for work. She'd gone to every real estate agent in all the surrounding beach towns. She stopped in at all the hotels in the area. She'd even asked at the Cranberry Bay Historic Train Depot if they might need a receptionist or ticket seller. But, the story was always the same. People would hire if they had more business. The real estate agents apologized, saying that second homes just weren't selling right now. The beach town hotel owners apologized and explained they were recovering from a couple seasons of low occupancy due to a series of unfortunate summer storms and a faltering economy. They didn't have money to pour into remodels of rooms and entryways. Her headache pulsed, and she gripped the edges of the park bench. Yesterday, she had visited the local bank and asked to open a home equity line of credit. But without a regular steady means of income, the bank declined her request.

Rylee tightened her grip on the cold wooden slates. She wouldn't give up. She couldn't give up. There had to be something she could do.

Rylee looked toward the row of two-story brick buildings that lined the riverfront walkway below the park's hillside. She remembered that there had been a candy store when she was a child, and she had selected different types of fudge from the glass cabinets. Chocolate almond had been her favorite. She always tucked a small package into her suitcase to eat on the plane ride back to Vegas. Now, darkened windows and storefront signs missing letters marred the buildings. A light flickered on in a small office at the end of the building with a real estate agent sign in the front.

Resolved, Rylee threw back her shoulders. If she couldn't get a job and was unable to secure a home equity line of credit, it was time to face selling her grandmother's home. The cost of the repairs could be taken out of the sale, or a buyer could be found for an "as-is" sale. She had to let go of her childhood dreams that her grandmother's home was worth a lot of money. She doubted any real estate agent in Portland was going to be interested in her grandmother's home. Rylee squared her shoulders and clenched her teeth. She'd have to use Bryan's real estate services.

Rylee headed down a narrow pathway leading out of the park and to the riverfront walkway. Raisin trotted beside her, his toenails clicking on the cement pavement and his tags jingling. A seagull circled above her and landed on the marina's ramshackle office building.

Rylee reached the last brick building and pushed open the small door. A steep and narrow staircase loomed in front of her. She grasped the banister and stepped up the stairs to a small door on the second floor. A "For Sale" sign rested against a wall. In large red lettering, it read "Cranberry Bay Real Estate. Bryan Shuster." Raisin whined beside her and tried to turn around in the dark space.

"It's okay, bud." Rylee petted the dog and reassured both the dog and herself that things were going to be okay. "We're just going to take care of some business." She wanted nothing more than to bolt.

Suddenly, the door jerked open and Bryan stood in the doorframe. The light behind him cast a glow around his muscular frame, and his blue jeans hugged his muscular legs. A green sweater stretched across his broad chest, and the heat surged in Rylee's face.

"Can I help you?"

"I'd like to list my grandmother's home." Rylee gripped Raisin's leash and willed herself not to run. Her heart pounded in her chest. It's just the sale of a house, she told herself, knowing full well that the sale of the house was not causing her surging emotions. It was the man standing in front of her.

"Not a problem." Bryan leaned against the doorframe. "We can get that done." He smiled at her, sending her heart crashing to her ribs. "I wanted to talk to you anyway."

Rylee could do nothing but nod, too afraid to speak and reveal her emotions.

"Are you interested in a job?"

Rylee swallowed hard, forcing herself to concentrate. "I would love a job. Who do I contact?"

"Me." Bryan's eyes glowed. "Is that okay?"

"You?" Rylee stared beyond Bryan into the small office. He couldn't expect her to work with him, could he? She'd never be able to be so close to him in his office and maintain an emotional and physical distance.

"I've just landed a listing. The owner would like it staged to sell. Is this something you could do?"

"Of course." Rylee straightened and thought she saw emotion cross Bryan's face. But before she could be sure she'd seen anything, it was gone. "I stage property. I did an entire condo building in Vegas. It was beautiful. My business partner and I worked for weeks on it. We used beautiful draperies and high-end furniture." She paused and laughed. "I wanted to buy one by the time we finished."

She flushed. Why had she gushed on to Bryan? He wasn't asking her for a job history. He was giving her a job without any references or previous work experience. Rylee slipped her left hand into her pocket and stepped back.

Bryan cleared his throat and shifted. "I was just going to look at the property now. You could come along?"

"Where is it?" Rylee nodded to Raisin. "I can drop him off at home on the way."

"We can walk. It's on the other side of the park, near the west bank of the river."

"A riverfront property?" Rylee frowned. "Is it one of the businesses near the marina?"

"Not exactly." Bryan cleared his throat. "It's the river cottages."

Rylee swallowed hard as heat filled her face. "The river cottages?" Grateful for the poorly lit stairwell, she lowered her eyes to the dirty doormat. On her twenty-first birthday, Bryan had brought her to the cottage. He'd set a small kitchen table with real china place settings borrowed from his mother. He'd cooked a wonderful meal of lasagna and thick French bread and made her a chocolate cake. Afterward, he proposed to her. That night, she believed she could marry him. She believed she could move to Cranberry Bay. She believed she'd find a way to keep her father out of harm's way in Vegas while she lived in Cranberry Bay. She believed it was possible to have her life in Cranberry Bay without telling the secret of his gambling addiction. She believed her world would come together perfectly. But everything changed the next day with one phone call from the Vegas police. Quietly, she packed her bags, knowing she'd never be able to marry Bryan and live in Cranberry Bay without betraying her long-held family secret. She'd never be able to leave her father without someone to take care of him.

Bryan stared into her eyes and sent her heart racing. "Will the location be a problem?"

"No." Rylee shook her head firmly. This was a business deal. She needed the job, and there wasn't time for sentimentality over the past. "It's not a problem for me. Is it a problem for you?"

Bryan's ears turned slightly pink, but he shook his head. "Not a problem for me. We should be able to attract a good buyer once the cottages are staged."

Rylee nodded. It didn't matter how she once felt about Bryan. That was in the past. Today all that mattered for both of them was getting the job done.

"Let me get my jacket." Bryan stepped into the room and grabbed his coat off a tall chair sitting in front of a desk. "We'll walk over to the cottages."

Rylee turned and headed down the narrow staircase. It was just business, she reminded herself. The job would give her the necessary means to secure the home equity line of credit, finish the work on her grandmother's house, and leave.

Outside, Rylee took a deep breath of the crisp night air. Cranberry Bay always smelled like a Christmas tree farm with the towering evergreen trees that surrounded it. She led Raisin to a small patch of grass on the side of the building. As soon as the bank opened tomorrow, she'd secure the loan. It was a small town, and Bryan would verify her employment. She'd still list the home with Bryan, but at least it wouldn't have to be sold "as-is." Rylee had seen what happened to the older homes in Vegas that were listed "as-is." Many of them were torn down to make room for apartment buildings. She didn't know about the zoning laws in Cranberry Bay, but she hated to think of someone tearing down her grandmother's beloved home.

"Ready?" Bryan stepped up beside her

"Yes." Rylee and Raisin easily stepped into pace beside Bryan.

The rain had stopped, and some of the clouds gave way to a blue sky with puffy white clouds. Walking with Bryan felt so familiar and comfortable that Rylee soon found herself telling him about some of the homes she had worked on over the years. She recounted stories of owners' demands and requests for furnishings which took her everywhere from estate sales to expensive home stores. The two of them were laughing by the time they reached the river rock path leading to the six cottages.

Rylee stopped. Time hadn't changed the brown-shingled cottages, which sat in a circle around a grassy area that held a couple of Adirondack chairs and a fire pit. The cottages all looked alike, with large picture windows, chimneys and wooden front doors. A small metal sign hung on the front of the first cottage. Rylee peered closer and could barely make out the letters: "Fishing."

Rylee slipped her hand into her pocket. She pulled out her cell phone and tapped notes into the small screen. "The first thing we'll want to do is buy flowers for a large pot at each door. Probably at this time of year there is nothing left, but I'll see if I can find something marked with a discount. There'll need to be curtains on the windows, and we'll want to leave them open and pulled back with a nice tie." She eyed the gravel walkway. "The path could use new gravel, but we won't worry about that for now. The important thing will be making each cottage have curb appeal."

"I can clear out the weeds." Bryan leaned over and yanked out a tall scraggly weed lodged in the gravel. "It should only take me a couple hours or so."

"I'll see what I can do about making up some new signs for each cottage. It shouldn't be hard to find some old boards and paint names on them to hang as signs for each cottage." Rylee continued to type fast notes into her phone.

Bryan leaned over and flipped up a doormat. He pulled out a small key. "I will have the locks rekeyed. Why don't you take this one for now? The same key fits every cottage."

Rylee took the key from Bryan, and his fingers touched hers. For a minute, neither of them moved. His eyes stared into hers, and she couldn't find her voice. She felt twenty-one again, in love with the boy she'd had a crush on since she was fifteen.

Bryan reached over, and, with his thumb, caressed the side of her face. "Rylee," he said. The longing in his eyes mirrored hers. Her chest ached with the unfilled promise of everything they'd left behind.

Rylee grabbed the key from Bryan and leaned down to pick up her cell phone. Her heart pounded as she inserted the key into the lock. She could not allow herself to remember the past. Not now. Not ever. Her hands shook as she inserted the key into the lock. She twisted the doorknob, but the door didn't open.

"Something is stuck," Rylee muttered. She leaned her shoulder against the door and pushed.

"Here." Bryan stepped up beside her. "Let me." His body brushed against hers, and she inhaled his spicy aftershave, sending her emotions back into overdrive.

Bryan grunted and pressed against the door as it swung open into a dark room. "I'll get these doors fixed as soon as possible."

Rylee followed Bryan into the cold room and shivered. A couple of used logs sat in the fireplace. The room was empty except for three folding chairs and a card table. Rylee stepped into the small kitchen area. A refrigerator, tucked into a red Formica countertop, clunked as if on its final legs. The small metal sink smelled of fish, and Rylee scrunched her nose.

"I'm sorry. "Bryan ran his finger along the dusty front window ledge "I haven't been inside any of these for years. I didn't realize the condition they'd be in. I'll tell Dennis we can't stage them, and I'll just try to sell them as-is."

"No. Wait. I think we can make this work." Rylee turned in a circle and studied the one-room cottage. "They're vintage cottages, and I'll use that as the theme." She pointed to the fireplace. "If it doesn't work, I'll place a set of candles in the middle. We can cover the fish scent with some good bleach. I'll bake some cookies to serve at an open house."

"Are you sure?" Bryan ran his hand through his hair. "This looks like a lot of work. And there are five others. I'm assuming they're all in the same state."

"I can do it." Rylee nodded. "Why don't we make a list of what needs to be done? There might be some things I can hire out. Is there a budget for the project?"

Bryan shifted his weight back and forth. "No." He lowered his voice. "I need you to keep something to yourself."

Rylee nodded. "Of course. Client confidentiality is important."

"Mrs. Perkins is ill. Dennis mentioned needing the money, so they could move to be closer to their grandchildren in California. I'm guessing it is also to cover her medical expenses."

"I'm sorry to hear that," Rylee said, softening toward Bryan. "I remember how much you cared about her."

"Yes." Bryan's voice cracked. "I do. The whole town loves her. I'm sure we could do a fund-raiser to help with her costs, but I doubt she'd accept it."

"The staging won't be a problem," Rylee said firmly. "I'll poke around in the antique shop and see if I can scout out a few thrift stores or garage sales. If needed, I'll head into Portland for the day and look around. We can get this done."

"Thank you," Bryan said. His blue eyes swam with emotion.

"Not a problem," Rylee said, her voice brisk as she resisted the urge to reach out and take Bryan's hand. "I've dealt with worse situations." She checked the time on her phone. "In fact, why don't I head over to Ivy's shop now? We'll put a colorful tag on anything that comes from her store, so prospective buyers know where to purchase the item."

"That's a great idea," Bryan said. "I'm going to stick my head into the other cottages, and I'll let you know how bad they look."

The boyish grin she loved broke across his face, and her heart cascaded in small flutters. For a minute, she couldn't move and felt the old swirl of joyful emotion in her stomach.

Raisin's sharp bark jerked her out of her thoughts. The dog had placed his paws on the window and pressed his nose against the glass. "Down." Rylee called Raisin to her side. She clipped his leash to his collar and stepped out the door. Her pulse raced. She needed to put distance between herself and Bryan. Rylee pulled her hood over her head and headed for Main Street.

By the time she had walked the three blocks, her pulse had returned to normal. The cool breeze whipped around the sides of the buildings and chilled her heated body.

In the doorway of the antique shop, Ivy struggled, trying to fit a large nightstand through the door. "Let me get that." Rylee stepped up to the glass door with "Antiques" etched in gold lettering on it.

"Thanks," Ivy said, as she and Rylee set the nightstand down in front of a large front counter. Light-green paint was chipped in the corners, and a bottom drawer missed a knob. Otherwise, everything looked in good condition. The piece would be perfect for a small table beside a thick couch in one of the cottages.

"What can I help you with?" Ivy wiped her hands on her jeans.

"I'd like that nightstand," Rylee said, and briefly explained her plan to stage the river cottages.

After she finished, Ivy waved her hand toward the vast store. "Feel free to look around for whatever you need. I'll be happy to donate some of this stuff. People use the store as a dumping ground for their old junk."

"Why don't you tell them the store doesn't accept the items?" Rylee asked, puzzled at Ivy's policy.

Ivy shrugged. "I'm too much of a softy to say no. I know what it's like to have an attic full of treasures you don't know what to do with." She lowered her voice as a shadow crossed her face. "The store helps people out, even if no one will ever buy the items. They have a place to keep those things that once were special."

"And if Cranberry Bay becomes the next big thing, people might want these things." Rylee said. She smiled at Ivy. She understood why Ivy chose to keep people's treasures, whether or not they could sell. She knew what it was like to have a houseful of things that had once been filled with meaning and purpose and had become only part of what they used to be.

"That would be great," Ivy said. "But until we get a reason for people to stay longer than an hour or two in Cranberry Bay, none of this stuff is going anywhere. I'm happy to let you take what you need."

Raisin nosed toward a tall stack of old records. Ivy held out her hand. "I'll keep Raisin up here. I had a dog for fifteen years. She saw me through everything. She passed away a few months ago, and I haven't had the heart to get another one." Ivy leaned down and rubbed Raisin's ears. "But I can borrow you, right buddy?"

Raisin leaned against Ivy's leg. Rylee grabbed a small wire basket from a stack by the counter. She headed toward the back of the store. She had learned it was best to start at the back and work her way forward, rather than moving in some random path. Some of the best deals often were at the back of thrift stores because people got too distracted by the things closer to the front.

Rylee passed a table filled with hand-stitched towels and pillowcases. She paused and scooped a couple into the bottom of her basket. The towels would look perfect hanging from the stove in the kitchen. She took another three steps and collided with a teen girl who ducked out of a small alcove filled with vintage dresses.

"Watch where you are going." The teen clutched a pink dress and a yellow teacup to her denim jacket.

"I'm sorry." Rylee apologized to the tall, gangly girl who looked to be about sixteen. "I didn't see you."

Rylee stepped beside a shelf filled with teacups and saucers that matched the one in the teen's hand. A vision of the tea set placed at a small table and covered with a lace tablecloth flashed across Rylee's mind. "Are you going to buy those?"

"I don't know." The girl hugged the teacup closer to her. "Why?"

"Because if you're not, I'd like them." Rylee hid the smile from her voice. She'd argued with plenty of experienced shoppers over items, but never a teenager who looked like the fiercest competitor she'd met.

"Yea?" The girl held the teacup up to the light. She ran her finger from the edge to the bottom of the cup. "It's got a crack down the center. Might be hard to drink tea out of this one."

Rylee's gaze followed the girl's finger. "You're right. You've got a good eye."

The girl shrugged, but her cheeks turned pink at the compliment. "I like to browse antique stores. I want to be a designer someday with my own shop."

"I'm Rylee Harper." Rylee stuck out her hand. "I'm an interior designer." The words felt good on her tongue. When was the last time she'd introduced herself as a designer? Not for at least the last six months. After she severed all ties to her former best friend and their business, she hadn't wanted to talk about her career to anyone.

"Maddie." The teen nodded in the direction of Rylee. "Are you working on something in Cranberry Bay?"

"I'm staging a set of vintage river cottages. It's just temporary while I get my grandmother's house sold."

"Do you need any help?" Maddie shifted back and forth on her feet. "I just landed in town and I could use a little work. I've got some money I owe people..."

"I could use some help." Rylee raised her eyebrows at the teen. She didn't want to probe too deeply, but the girl was obviously hurting over something. "But I can't pay you. Do you need school credits?"

When she'd been in business with Ericka, they'd often had a young person helping them. The teens earned credits for working in real-world jobs, and they gained extra hands to help out with the grunt work.

"Yea." Maddie gazed at the floor. "I could use some of those too."

"Great!" Rylee said, surprised at how easy the conversation had been and even more surprised at the hope that rose in her chest. It felt good to help someone again. She'd do a quick check on Maddie with Ivy or Katie and make sure everything was okay. In a small town like Cranberry Bay, someone would know Maddie and could fill in the details. "Why don't you grab another basket, and we'll see what we can fill up. I'm focusing on designing each cottage around a different color. The first one is going to be light yellow."

After an hour of searching, laughing, and exclaiming over everything from rotary phones to shoes missing their other half, Ivy, Maddie, and Rylee stood around a large stack of chairs, end tables, dishes, and linens.

"I don't know." Ivy nodded to a pair of broken dining room chairs. "A lot of this looks pretty beat up to me. I can't even believe I took it into the store. You're really doing me a favor, but I can't imagine how you're going to use some of this in those cottages."

"A coat of paint can make everything fresh again." Rylee finished tagging a pair of antique bedside tables with a heavy cardstock circle with the store's logo.

"I'm good with painting," Maddie said. "I helped on the sets for my school's play in Seattle last spring."

"Great!" Rylee said and smiled at her. "We'll add painting to your list."

The front door chimed. "Hello! Anyone behind all this stuff?" Bryan said.

Rylee maneuvered her way through the pile of dishes and chairs. She wiped her hands on her pants and scanned the stack. "I think we made good progress today. I can set up at least three of the cottages and check the area for local estate or garage sales."

Bryan ran his finger along the edges of a rusty folding chair. "Are you sure this is going to work? It looks like it should be in the trash."

"We're going to paint it, Uncle Bryan." Maddie stepped around the corner of a large basket stacked with plastic picnic dishes. "I'm going to paint all the chairs."

Rylee whirled around to face Bryan. Bryan was Maddie's uncle? She quickly tried to recover from her surprise and said, "We'll add a new cushion and some burlap ribbon tied on the back. Everything can be made to have a purpose, even things that appear broken."

"Yes," Bryan said, holding Rylee's gaze. "Everything can be made to have a purpose."

Rylee flushed as Bryan broke her gaze and turned to Maddie. "Where is your Mom?" Bryan asked Maddie.

"She's at the grocery store." Maddie frowned. "She said I could browse the shop, and I ran into Rylee."

Rylee smiled at the intricate connections of Cranberry Bay. Maddie was Bryan's twin sister's daughter. Lisa would have no problems with Maddie working with her to help Bryan. Quickly she stepped in between Bryan and Maddie. "Maddie was helping me. She's going to be my assistant and earn either credit hours or volunteer work time."

Bryan touched Rylee's arm. He lowered his voice. "Did she tell you why she's here?"

"No." Rylee frowned. She was usually a good judge of character. Maddie seemed like a girl who just needed a new direction, similar to herself right now. She glanced over at Maddie, whose frown had deepened.

Bryan lowered his face to whisper against Rylee's cheek. "She served some time in the juvenile detention center. Lisa wanted her out of Seattle for a while. If you want to back out…"

"No," Rylee said, straightening and pushing aside the butterfly feelings that arose when Bryan breathed against her cheek. "Maddie knows how to pick a good item from a bad one, and that's what counts in my book." She smiled at Maddie.

Maddie watched them. Rylee hoped the girl knew everything would be okay. She wasn't going to judge her on the past.

"Everyone deserves a second chance." Rylee looked up into Bryan's eyes.

Bryan held her gaze. His face darkened with emotion. "Yes." Bryan touched her hand. "They do."

Chapter Eight

Bryan strode to the river cottages. A bakery bag, filled with two turkey-and-cranberry sandwiches and creamy tomato soup, bumped against his leg. Carefully, he shifted the sack to his other hand, being sure not to tip the covered soup cups over. Sasha had even convinced him to toss in a couple of her oatmeal raisin cookies, winking at him and telling him it would sweeten his lunch with Rylee. He didn't need much to sweeten his feelings, and had to keep reminding himself his goal was to convince her to stay in Cranberry Bay, not to fall in love with her again.

Bryan rounded the corner and stopped. An old wheelbarrow filled with colorful pots of fall mums sat in the center of the yard between the cottages. A tall scarecrow wearing a green scarf leaned against the outer wall of cottage number one. Colorful lawn chairs were placed around a stack of wood sitting inside the fire pit. Outside each cottage, orange and yellow fall mums were planted inside burlap bags and tied with colorful ribbons. Festive fall wreaths made of leaves hung from each of the cottage doors. New hand-painted signs hung from bright ribbon on a small nail at the front of each cottage.

Rylee was hanging a set of curtains in the large picture window of the middle cottage. Bryan set the bakery bags on a green picnic table. He strode toward the middle cottage, unable to stop the grin from spreading across his face. In less than a week, Rylee had

89

brought the cottages to life. As soon as he snapped some pictures and posted them on the listing service, buyers would be calling his office in droves. This was exactly what people wanted. They didn't want run-down cottages they'd have to fix up. Buyers wanted cottages they could walk into and call their own without the headache of doing the skillful and thoughtful work Rylee and Maddie had pulled together in days.

Rylee knocked on the window and motioned to him.

Bryan pushed open the door. "You've done an amazing job!"

"I've still got a lot of work to do," Rylee muttered, her mouth struggling to move around a large screw she held between her teeth. She stood on the middle rung of a small ladder. Raisin lay on a small fleece blanket beside the kitchen table. He lifted his head at Bryan and wagged his tail.

"Hey buddy." Bryan nodded to Raisin without taking his eyes off Rylee.

"Can you grab that bracket?" Rylee pointed to the windowsill as the ladder wobbled.

"I've got it." Bryan picked up the hook, handed it to Rylee and wrapped his fingers around the steel ladder. His fingers brushed against her ankles, and he inhaled the familiar scent of her perfume, jasmine vanilla. He was transported to the summer nights they had snuggled in each other's arms and listened to the summer concert series in the park.

"I'm just about done here." Rylee placed the drill bit against the wall. As she stretched forward, her foot slipped, and she slid down two steps of the ladder toward Bryan.

"I've got you." He wrapped his arms around her.

She squirmed around to face him. Her eyes widened, and her cheeks flushed. But she didn't try to move out of his arms.

"That was a close one." He drew light circles on her back. Bryan stared into Rylee's eyes and swirled with emotions he'd spent years pushing away.

Rylee parted her mouth, and without thinking, Bryan lowered his face to touch her lips. But before he reached her, someone said: "Anyone here?"

Startled, Bryan broke away from Rylee. "Hey Dennis." Bryan cleared his throat and tried to pretend he hadn't just been caught kissing the girl of his long-ago summer childhood dreams.

Raisin shook himself and stood. He wandered to Dennis and nosed against his palm.

Dennis petted the dog and grinned. "Sorry. I didn't mean to interrupt anything."

"You're not." Rylee stepped away from Bryan. She smoothed her hands over her jeans. "What can we do for you? Would you like to see the cottages? They're not quite ready, but we'd be happy to show you one or two."

Rylee was talking so fast, Bryan couldn't help but think she was just as nervous about being caught with her lips near Bryan's as he had been. They were both grown adults, and yet something about kissing Rylee Harper made him feel sixteen again.

"Dennis." Bryan said to cover the awkwardness. "I'm sorry. You remember Rylee Harper. She's back in town selling her grandmother's place. I've hired her to help stage the cottages for the sale."

"Oh!" Rylee's face reddened. "I'm sorry. I didn't recognize you. I thought you might be someone who was interested in buying."

"No worries. I can see the two of you are busy." Dennis said, and smiled. "My wife, Allison, wanted me to drop these off." He motioned toward a large box by the door. "There are some dishes in there. Picnic baskets. That type of thing. She thought you might want it for the staging." He looked around the cottage. "But it looks like you've got things wrapped up. Everything looks great."

Rylee scurried to the box and flipped open the top. She pulled out a set of red plastic dishes and a large picnic basket. "These are perfect. I'll set them out in the first cottage. They will really add to the gingham curtains Katie is sewing."

"Great," Dennis said. "I'll tell Allison they will work perfectly." He nodded to Bryan. "I'll stop by and pick up the rest of the things from the sixth cottage on Monday."

Dennis stepped out the door, and Rylee busied herself digging inside her large shoulder bag. "I don't know about you, but I'm starving. I tucked a granola bar in here this morning." She stuck her face in the bag. "If I find it, I can split it with you."

"No, need," Bryan said. "I brought lunch. Will you join me?"

Raisin walked over to Bryan. He gazed up at him with wide eyes as if he knew the word lunch.

Bryan smiled at Raisin and his heart pounded. It'd be easy for Rylee to say no. Lunch was not part of their working relationship, and the kiss they'd almost shared didn't make things easier. It was a working relationship. He'd been out of line to try and kiss her. She'd have every right to turn and walk away, but he hoped she'd stay.

Rylee dropped her purse onto the table and shrugged. "Lunch would be nice. I can't find the granola bar. I must have left it on the counter at Grandma's house. I'll just wash off a few of these plates and be right out."

"I'll help you." Bryan stepped into the small kitchen. Raisin followed him and sat down beside a kitchen chair. Bryan grabbed a white embroidered towel hanging on the stove.

"Not that one." Rylee opened the top kitchen drawer and pulled out a thick yellow dishtowel. "Use this one."

Bryan carefully folded the special towel and placed it back on the stove. "My Mom does the same thing," he said. "At Christmas, we can never use the towels she sets out. They're for decoration."

"I know it's a silly thing." Rylee ran the water and tested it with her finger before slipping a couple of plates and two glasses under the faucet. She dropped globs of dish soap into the sink and stirred the water with her hand. "But Maddie picked these out. I'm not sure how much washing they can stand with the embroidery."

"Maddie." Bryan wiped his hands on the towel. He shifted his weight and looked at the ground, then up at Rylee. "Honestly, I don't know what to do about her. I want to help her, but I don't know how." He cleared his throat. It was never easy for him to admit he didn't know how to do something, especially when it came to matters involving his family.

Rylee handed him a clean plate. Her quiet acceptance filled the room as Bryan toweled a plate. He'd always loved the way she listened.

"Maddie's had a hard time. Her Dad died when she was young. Lisa has never quite been able to afford a home in Seattle. They've moved around a lot, different apartments and neighborhoods. I wish they'd come back to Cranberry Bay, but Lisa says the town is just too small for her. She loves the city."

Bryan looked out the small window above the sink as a bird darted to a branch on a nearby Japanese maple.

"Maddie loves working on the cottages." Rylee placed a glass on the counter. Water dripped around the edges. "She really has a good eye for everything she picks out and puts together. I think she has a gift for design."

Bryan exhaled. He lifted the glass and ran his towel over the edges. "That's good to hear because it's hard to figure out what she wants to do right now. The last time we saw Maddie, she was a cheerful girl who kept us all laughing during a very hard time for our family. But now she's sullen and withdrawn."

Rylee placed another plate on the counter. She reached in and lifted the drain, allowing the water to run out of the sink. "There was a summer I came to visit when Grandma and Grandpa might have said the same thing about me." Rylee turned and leaned against the counter. "Mom had just died, and I was furious she could be taken from us so suddenly."

Bryan studied Rylee. He knew her mother had died, but she'd never talked about it with him. She'd never talked much about any of her family, except for her grandparents. At twenty-one, he had figured they had plenty of time, and she would talk to him in time. He also had to admit that he'd been selfish and didn't understand the importance of listening to the other person, too. It'd taken a few years with his ex-wife for the lesson to sink in. Now he found himself eagerly waiting to show her how well he could listen to her, too. He wanted to know more about the girl who had grown up to be the strong and hard-working woman who stood before him.

"Grandma and Grandpa tried everything. Trips to the ice cream store, fishing with Grandpa, crafts, even a trip to Portland. But no matter what they did, nothing worked."

"Until..." Bryan prompted.

Rylee smiled shyly at him. "This boy came to work with Grandpa in the garage. They liked to fiddle with cars."

"Me?" Bryan pointed his index finger at his chest. He flushed, but he smiled broadly.

Rylee grinned. "Yes. When you came to work with Grandpa, my anger disappeared. Grandma thought it'd be good if I could learn to cook that summer, and she taught me how to bake cookies."

"Which you served to me." Bryan wrinkled his nose. "And some sugary lemonade."

"You never said you didn't like my lemonade." Rylee nudged Bryan's hip playfully.

"Well..." Bryan said. "It had a lot of sugar in it."

"It's okay," Rylee said, and laughed. "It was horrible, but everyone pretended to like it."

"So you think I should find a boy for Maddie to be interested in?" Bryan placed the two plates in the picnic basket.

"Not necessarily. I think she will come out of her shell, eventually. She seems to really like the vintage and antique shopping. She helped me pick out a lot of the pillows and colors in the cottages."

"I agree with you." Bryan closed the basket top. "And most importantly, no boy." He suspected Lisa would agree with him.

"No?" Rylee said, and laughed.

Her laughter danced along the cedar walls of the small cottage and filled Bryan's heart with a joy he hadn't allowed himself to feel for a long time. "Why don't we take our lunch to the river? It's a really nice day. Probably one of the last before the winter storms roll in."

"That sounds like a great idea." Rylee grabbed her coat from the peg behind the door. "But just in case the weather turns, I am prepared this time."

Bryan grinned. She sounded exactly like she always had whenever he'd take her out in Sawyer's motorboat. Bryan had never worried about getting cold, not as a native to the cold and damp summers of the Oregon coast. He dressed in layers. As the weather heated up, he and everyone else shed the layers, or they added them as the weather cooled down in the evenings. But Rylee never seemed to have the standard layers of T-shirts and fleece sweatshirts. Most of the time, she wore his sweatshirt or jacket.

Now Rylee pulled on a thick, black coat. She clipped Raisin's leash to his collar and smiled at him. "Ready."

The two walked the half-a-block to the park and settled on one of the picnic tables facing the river. Raisin positioned himself under Rylee's feet, close enough to be able to scoop any crumbs which might fall from lunch. In the spring, the park pathway was lined with colorful tulips and daffodils, while pink and blue hydrangeas bloomed nearby. Couples often stopped at the small memorial bench to snap photos of each other. The river ran beside the park and provided a place for both fishing and lazy summer rafting. Today, the muddy waters gushed at a fast clip and filled the banks.

"The river is gushing pretty high, isn't it?" Rylee frowned at the deep water.

"We've just had some heavy rains. It's usually like this during the fall and winter." Bryan set the basket on the table and tossed one leg over the bench.

"Do the cottages ever flood?" Rylee stared into the water.

"I don't think so." Bryan tried to remember if Dennis had mentioned anything about flooded cottages. "We really haven't had a big flood since I was in high school."

"But it's been raining a lot."

"No more than usual." Bryan said, and chuckled. "You always visited in the summer. This is what late fall is like out here. Rain all the time."

"Mmm…" Rylee turned and sat down opposite him at the table. She reached into the picnic basket and pulled out a light-blue patchwork tablecloth.

Bryan fingered the corner. "This looks familiar."

"It was my grandmother's. She kept it on their back patio table during the summer." Rylee thumbed the edges of the cotton material. "It's a little threadbare. But it fit nicely with the colors in the cottage. I'm going to place it on the table in cottage number one."

"Rylee," Bryan said. His voice lowered. "You didn't have to do that. Please. You don't have to use your grandmother's things in the cottages. I can take you to estate sales or garage sales or we can check with my Mom and look in her attic."

"I know," Rylee said, her voice fragile and filled with emotion. "But it's okay. I'm going to sell Grandma's house in January. I can't take all of this with me to San Diego. I'm happy to use it in the cottages. When someone buys them, I'll be glad to give it away."

At the mention of San Diego, Bryan's heart dropped down to the soles of his thick boots. Nothing had changed. Rylee still wanted out of Cranberry Bay, just like she always had. She didn't see the job as leading to something else. She saw it as a way to fix her grandmother's home to sell. It was only his foolish heart that had let him get carried away with romantic ideas.

Bryan turned away from Rylee. He busied himself with taking out the soup and sandwiches. "How are the plans going for San Diego?"

"Everything is on target. Thanks to your recommendation letter to the bank, the loan for Grandma's house repairs came through. They'll be doing the work in December. I have set up three interviews in California for the beginning of January. One of the companies was very interested and wanted me to come early, but I want to stay and monitor the repairs."

Bryan's heartbeat spiked. By January, the bet with Sawyer would be lost. The riverboats would go to another town. Cranberry Bay would continue to shrink and die until there was nothing left of the town he loved. Bryan clenched his jaw. He had no choice. He had to tell her about the bet. If he told her about it, maybe they could pretend she was staying, at least long enough for him to get the money from Sawyer. Then she could go on her way. "Rylee," Bryan began. "There's something…"

Rylee swung to face him, and her lips parted slightly. He couldn't think of anything but how much he wanted to kiss those lips. He wanted to finish the kiss they'd started in the cottages. The river rushed beside them, and a seagull's cry echoed from a distant roof.

Bryan traced his finger lightly down her neck.

She let out a small sigh and closed her eyes.

"Rylee." Her name filled his mind and was warm on his lips.

She tilted her head upward, and his lips met hers. He wrapped his arms around her and kissed her, deeply.

Chapter Nine

A truck engine roared on the highway above the river park. Rylee pulled out of the kiss. She placed her hand against Bryan's broad chest. "I can't…" she broke off and turned away. She couldn't go there. She couldn't risk the hurt it would bring to both of them to rekindle their love when she could never promise to stay in Cranberry Bay.

Quickly, she busied herself with picking up their plates and napkins and scooping all of the remnants into the wicker basket.

"Let me help." Bryan reached for the picnic tablecloth at the same time as she did. Their fingers touched. His thumb caressed her hand. "Nothing has changed," he said.

"No," Rylee said. "Nothing has changed." The words tore into her. Nothing had changed about how she felt about Bryan, and his kiss only verified what she'd known all along. She'd tried to put all her feelings behind her. She'd convinced herself she loved Matt and became engaged to one of Vegas's top hotel owners. He had known about her father, and he hadn't cared. Her father was one of his clients at his private gambling parties. But in her heart she knew the truth. She'd never loved Matt the way she loved Bryan. It'd taken just one kiss to show her how much she still loved Bryan. She squared her shoulders, but nothing had changed in her decision either. She had to sell her grandmother's house and leave Cranberry Bay. She had to do it to protect her father. He needed her more than Bryan, and she couldn't leave him.

"Okay." Bryan nodded and firmed his jaw. "Mind if Sawyer and I stop by this afternoon to take a look at those tools in your grandfather's garage? I want to get those out of the house before we start showing it to potential buyers. When people know it's an estate sale, they'll try to ask for anything in the home."

"Not a problem." Rylee slipped the folded tablecloth on top of the dishes in the picnic basket. She shut the lid and twisted the gold clasp, keeping her gaze averted from Bryan. "The sewing circle meets this afternoon. Do you know the code for the key box on the side of the garage?"

"It's your birthday." Bryan's eyes searched hers. "I remember your birthday, Rylee."

Bryan's words sent shivers racing into Rylee's stomach, and she looked into his eyes. The confusion she felt was mirrored back to her from his eyes. The two of them gazed at each other, not saying a word. Her birthday fell on the final day of August. It was always the last day of her summer visits, and Bryan brought flowers, freshly picked pink and yellow roses from his Mom's garden. "See you next summer," he'd say, and lean down to kiss her. Afterward, he always said, "The last kiss has to be good. It has to keep us until I see you next June."

"Ready?" Bryan lifted the picnic basket off the table.

"Yes." Rylee swallowed hard. The sailboat masts chimed from the nearby marina. Their first real date had been on one of the sailing boats. A longtime family friend of Bryan's gave him use of the boat for the evening. They'd cruised into a small alcove on the other side of the bay and docked alongside a floating buoy.

The waves rocked against the boat as they had kissed for the first time. The pain cut through Rylee's chest. Everywhere she looked in Cranberry Bay, another memory of Bryan confronted her.

"Do you want me to take Raisin back to the house? It'd be easier than taking him to Katie's shop?"

"Yes. Thank you. But, he can be hard to walk sometimes. He jerks on the leash and tries to pull you along. If you take it slow with him he does fine."

"I got it covered." Bryan said. He reached over and took the leash from Rylee's hand. Their fingers brushed against each other. "Trust me."

Rylee nodded. Trust. That was the problem. She'd done everything on her own for so long, it was so hard to let someone do a simple thing for her.

Raisin trotted by Bryan's side and when they reached the cottages, Rylee hurried into the middle building and picked up her notes and a piece of fabric. She dropped it all into her bag and grabbed her cell phone from the kitchen counter. She frowned at the missed call. Quickly, she scrolled through the call list and her face paled.

"What is it?"

"Nothing." Rylee shook her head. "I'm sure it's nothing." There was no message, but there didn't need to be. The familiar number of her father's latest apartment told her all she needed. He'd either lost money, or he was on a high after winning big. Either way, the call wasn't good news. "I'll touch base with you tomorrow about the cottages. I should have it wrapped up in a few days." Rylee's voice was brisk and businesslike.

Before Bryan could respond, Rylee hurried out the door and headed down the street toward the New Leaf Sewing Shop. She hadn't talked to her Dad since receiving the news she'd inherited her grandmother's home. The lawyer's letter was mailed to both her father and her. Dad called minutes after receiving it. Rylee tried to calm him, but it'd been no use. He'd counted on the inheritance of the home to help feed his gambling debts. As always, Rylee was torn. Torn between wanting to help her father by giving him the money from the sale of the house or using it to restart her own life.

Rylee had offered him a place to live in San Diego. She suggested they buy a two-bedroom home to share, knowing it would be her income that would contribute to the household expenses. Dad told her he needed to research a few job opportunities, but the plan sounded like a good one, and he'd always wanted to learn how to bet the horse races. Now Rylee only hoped the sale of the house would give them enough money to buy something for the two of them. Homes in San Diego were not cheap, and it didn't look like her grandmother's house was going to net very much income on the sale.

Rylee pushed away her worries and pulled open the door of the New Leaf Sewing Shop. A small bell chimed above her head. The smell of cinnamon and laughter filled the room.

"Hello!" Katie called from the back table. She and Ivy leaned over a thick pattern book.

In the middle of the shop, Lisa browsed shelves filled with red and green cotton fabric. She added a bolt to her stack in the cart. Her blue eyes, so like Bryan's, met Rylee's. "I just love all this holiday fabric," Lisa said, and sighed. "I have no idea how I'll ever sew this many aprons before Christmas, but I can't stop myself."

"I'm sorry I'm late." Rylee apologized to Katie. She set her bag on the long wooden cutting table.

No worries." Katie said. "Ivy is still picking her pattern, and Lisa is buying out the holiday fabrics. Sasha and Gracie are looking for the perfect matching thread. Do you need anything?"

Rylee reached into her bag and pulled out two yards of pink-and-yellow cotton fabric. She'd found the material in her grandmother's sewing closet along with various spools of matching thread. "I'd like to use this if that's okay. I have the thread, but I don't have a pattern."

Katie picked up a corner of the fabric and moved her fingers over the edges. Her voice softened. "I remember when your grandmother bought this piece. It was a couple years ago. I had a special on spring fabrics. The fabrics didn't sell very well. I always suspected your grandmother was buying the material to help me."

Rylee's throat tightened. She'd often seen her grandmother make similar gestures in other stores. She always asked which items weren't selling and then bought at least one of them, even if she already owned it. Rylee smiled, thinking about the time Grandma bought three flour sifters from the Cranberry Bay hardware and grocery store.

Gracie walked up to the table, her long hair curling halfway down her back. "Which one do you think would be best?" She held out three spools of green cotton thread.

Sasha stepped up behind her. At barely five feet, she was the shortest of all the women, but her boisterous laugh and attitude more than made up for it. "I told her the darker green would look the best with her fabric."

"Good eye." Katie nodded. Her voice took on an edge of authority. She straightened her thin shoulders. "It can be fun to change the thread out for every project and mix and match the bobbin and top thread. But sometimes you want to use the same color."

"Right." Lisa dumped three bolts of fabric on the cutting table. "I'm more interested in this gorgeous fabric and want to sew as many aprons as I can."

"In cases like this," Katie lowered her voice as if about to share the world's best secret. The women gathered closer. "it's best to know that certain thread colors can be used and not show. Lavenders and gray work very well for your lighter-colored fabrics while a navy or black will work best for your darker colors."

"When do we sew?" Ivy asked. She sounded very much like an excited twelve-year-old.

"First, we need to cut out the patterns." Katie said, and laughed at Ivy's impatience.

Ivy pushed the pattern book to Rylee. "I've picked mine." She pointed to a pretty ruffled waist apron in the left corner of the page. "I love ruffles."

"I need to choose a pattern, too." Lisa picked up a thick book of patterns and dropped it next to Rylee's book. "Since I have so much fabric, it'd probably be best to select an easy, basic pattern and do a lot of them all at once."

Rylee absently flipped through pages of dresses, shirts, and bags. She stopped on a colorful spread of dog beds and small T-shirts for dogs. Rylee considered the dog bed. It didn't look too challenging, and Raisin would love a new bed. Rylee couldn't help but think of Bryan. Would he know Raisin liked a small treat when he came home from a walk?

"Rylee?" Lisa touched her arm.

"Sorry." Rylee flushed. "I got a little distracted." She quickly flipped through a section of children's clothing patterns until she came to a page filled with colorful vintage aprons. Easily, she selected a vintage pattern with a scoop neckline and drop waist.

Ivy stepped up beside her. She opened a pattern and dumped out tissue paper pieces in a heap. "Katie and I have been talking, and we were thinking it might be fun to host a holiday market this year. We'd have to get approval from the council, but it would give Cranberry Bay a needed boost of activity in the winter months. If it went well, we could consider a spring or summer one too."

"Great idea." Lisa waved her hand over the bolts of fabric lying around her. "A holiday market would give me a place to sell all these aprons I want to make."

"Where would it be held?" Rylee asked. She'd been to a lot of different types of markets, always seeking out the perfect item for an elaborately furnished home. They were always fun, and she enjoyed the challenge of finding the right item.

"I have an old barn on the outskirts of town." Katie slipped a pin through the left side of a tissue paper pattern. "I'd love to fix it up and rent it out for large events—markets, weddings."

"Perfect idea! I could sell vintage baked goods," Sasha said. "Lemon icebox cake, homemade caramels, and butterscotch cream roll-ups."

"What a fabulous idea." Gracie echoed. "The River Rock Inn could be one of the sponsors and offer special discounts to vendors and visitors attending."

"I'd be happy to do the marketing," Lisa said, and frowned. "I'm not sure how long Maddie and I will be in town, but at least through the New Year."

"I'd love to work on the lay-out of the booths," Rylee added, swept up in the festive planning filling the cozy sewing shop. "I can help the vendors with an old-fashioned style."

Her mind spun with the possibilities of evergreen garlands draped from the rafters and pine cones set out in metal containers, all tied with holiday ribbon. She'd never been in Cranberry Bay during the holidays and could imagine the town became like a Christmas card, with all of the tall evergreens. Sudden warmth filled her at the idea of Cranberry Bay for the holidays. Her holidays were usually filled with work and large, expensive parties that left her empty. Maybe it wasn't so bad that the work on her grandmother's home would take longer than she thought.

"Of course we can wear our aprons!" Sasha said. "We'll set up an area to sell aprons too. People love holiday aprons." She twirled in a circle and waved her uncut harvest fabric in the air like a flag.

"Rylee!" Ivy gasped. "I almost forgot to tell you. I have fabulous news."

Rylee turned and smiled at Ivy's excited face.

"Colleen Sanders stopped into the shop today. She was on the way to her family's beach house on the coast. Her family owns the Beach and Sky Hotel."

"That's the big one," Gracie said, her voice darkening. "It has ten floors, and all the rooms have balconies and ocean views. They host an annual pet show on the beach every fall. It raises money for the local humane society."

"That's about the only good thing they do." Katie mumbled.

"Well," Ivy said, ignoring both Katie and Gracie's lackluster responses. "Colleen wanted to know about the cottages. She wants to interview you for the next edition of her magazine."

"What?" Rylee dropped her scissors on the table with a loud thump. Her heart pounded. An article in a national magazine would be just what she needed to get her career back on track.

"Yes." Ivy nodded. "She knew all about your design work in Vegas. I told her you have taken Maddie as a mentee. She wanted to include her in the story."

"Wait a minute," Lisa said firmly. "I don't want Maddie in an article. There's been some things which have happened." She tightened her lips and shook her head. "I don't think it's a good idea."

"Okay," Ivy said to Lisa. "Rylee can tell Colleen to leave that part of the story out. But the best part was Colleen recognized your name. You dropped off a business card at the hotel her family owns?"

"Yes," Rylee said. She rubbed her forehead, trying to remember what the Beach and Sky had told her. "I dropped off business cards at all the hotels on the coast. No one had any work."

"Well, the Beach and Sky does now. Colleen's brother runs the place and keeps a tight fist on everything. But her father recently died, and she's inherited half of the hotel. She wants to have a whole new look. She wants it to be more casual, with a touch of the old-fashioned. A vintage beach hotel like your cottages."

Rylee felt like she couldn't breathe. A job. No, not just any job. A big, important, career job had just landed in her lap as well as the opportunity to be featured in a national magazine. She never dreamed all of this good news could happen, here, in small-town Cranberry Bay. She thought jobs like this one only came along in large cities. Her mouth dried, and she swallowed hard. "How do I get in touch with her?"

"I've got her card and home cell number." Ivy reached into the side pocket of a large canvas bag hanging on the back of a chair. "Here you go." She held out an ivy card with black cursive lettering.

Rylee's hands shook as the familiar ring on her cell phone twinkled out of her bag.

"Phone call?" Katie called as all four women stopped and listened.

"Sorry. It's mine." Rylee grabbed the phone. Her father's number scrolled across the top. "Excuse me."

"You can go in the back room." Katie motioned toward a small door at the back of the store.

Rylee strode to the backdoor, stepped inside, and shut it. "Dad?" Rylee leaned her head against the wall. A bulletin board with neatly written index cards and a calendar lined one entire wall. Scraps of fabric were piled high on a folding table.

"Rylee, baby!" Her Dad's voice crackled, higher than a kite on his latest win. Rylee groaned to herself. She wasn't sure which was worse, Dad winning or Dad losing. She'd known the pattern all her life, and each cycle caused a sense of dread.

"...coming to visit Cranberry Bay."

"What?" Rylee shook her head. She hadn't heard right. Dad didn't say he wanted to visit Cranberry Bay. He hadn't been back in over thirty-five years. This wasn't the time to return.

"I'm coming to visit Cranberry Bay," Dad repeated. "I thought it'd be great for us to spend Thanksgiving together."

"You can't," Rylee blurted. If her father returned, he risked what all of them had worked so hard to do— keep his gambling addiction a secret. Dad couldn't go a day without finding some means to gamble, whether it was setting up a poker table or online or playing the Vegas tables. It would only take one poker game in Cranberry Bay for him to reveal what had happened to the hometown boy. "Grandma's house is under repair. There's nowhere to sleep. I'm sleeping on the couch." It wasn't true, but her father didn't need to know that.

"That's fine," Dad said. "There's a hotel in the area. The important thing is for us to be together for Thanksgiving. You know how I feel, baby; we're all we have. We have to stick together."

Rylee's heart contracted. Her father had always danced in and out of her life during the holiday season. He'd show up at her doorstep, unshaven and broke, looking for a place to sleep and a hot meal. Once she'd sought counseling, and the therapist told her to send him to the men's mission down the street. But she never had the heart to do it. Instead, she opened her home to him.

"Why don't we talk about this in a couple days? I'm right in the middle of something." In a couple days, Dad would have lost the money to travel. It was the boom and bust of his addiction, and the only thing she could count on.

"Sure, baby girl. We're going to celebrate a good old-fashioned Thanksgiving. It'll be great to reconnect with everyone in Cranberry Bay again. You know they loved me once."

"I know, Dad," Rylee said, her voice dropped to a whisper. "I know." Everyone adored her father. It was why all of them had worked for years to keep his addiction a secret from the town. Her heart ached, the way it always did after every conversation. She couldn't let the whole town see what her grandparents had tried so hard to keep secret over the years. Her Dad, the hometown star, had not succeeded. He was living off handouts from his daughter.

Slowly, Ryle clicked the phone off.

Katie stuck her head into the room. "What's the matter? You look like you've seen a ghost."

"It's okay," Rylee said, smiling to cover her rocketing emotions exactly the way she had for years. She followed Katie back into the sewing shop, where the chatter had turned to talk of Ivy's friendship with the high school history teacher and historic train conductor. Grateful to have someone else take center stage, Rylee turned toward the tall file cabinet of patterns. She pulled open the bottom drawer and hunted for the apron patterns in the back of the cabinet. But before she located the apron pattern, a sharp, familiar bark caused Rylee to straighten and look through the shop's large front window.

Bryan waved and smiled at her. Beside him, Raisin lunged on his leash toward the shop door.

Rylee dropped her pattern and hurried toward the door.

Chapter Ten

Bryan shifted the leash to his left hand as Rylee burst through the sewing shop door, bringing with her colors of joy on a gray, drizzling, and breezy late afternoon. Bryan's heart lifted.

"Is everything okay?" She kneeled beside Raisin and ran her hand over his fur.

"Everything's fine." Bryan placed his hand on her left shoulder. He squeezed lightly and felt her thin shoulder bones under his fingers. "They were tearing apart your grandmother's backyard, and there wasn't much room for Raisin to stretch out. I thought he'd like a walk."

"Tearing apart the yard?" Rylee jerked to an upright position and crossed her hands over her chest. Her eyes narrowed.

"Something about a pipe leak. Jim said he talked to you about it the other day."

A car drove down Main Street. Bryan stepped alongside Rylee and sheltered her from the passing car's water spray.

"Another problem with the house," Rylee muttered.

"Sorry," Bryan said. "Jim didn't tell you? The whole town uses an old version of copper pipes. Mom had hers replaced a few years ago. I think the city offered a grant to replace them. I can check to see if that's still available for you."

"Anything would help," Rylee said, her voice filled with strained emotion. "I never dreamed I'd find so many problems before I could sell."

"Maybe she didn't want you to sell," Bryan said.

"Why do you think that? Did she tell you?" Rylee's face screwed up tightly, the same way she used to look when she tried to work a puzzle piece at her grandmother's kitchen table.

Bryan twisted Raisin's leash tighter. He'd let his emotions slip out. He didn't want her to sell the house and leave Cranberry Bay. He needed Rylee to stay, not only for the bet, but because everything became a little happier, a littler lighter when she was around. "She didn't say anything," Bryan said. "I'm sure she wanted you to sell it." He hoped his voice didn't give away his emotions.

Katie tapped lightly on the large picture window and motioned to Rylee. Rylee nodded to her. "I'll grab my things and walk back with you and Raisin. I might as well find out what's going on with the backyard sooner rather than later."

Rylee hurried inside, and Bryan paced back and forth on the sidewalk with the dog by his side. The afternoon at Rylee's grandmother's home hadn't gone very well. He'd received a phone call from the riverboat real estate agent. Another bid had come in. A bid that was higher than Bryan's. If he wanted the casino boats, he had to increase his offer. Bryan raised his bid and promised the sale of the cottages would give him the rest of the needed money. But the cottages weren't receiving any attention. He'd posted pictures of the renovated and staged buildings, but so far, not a single bite.

Bryan fisted his left hand. A gust of wind whistled around the building. He stepped under the long, overhanging eaves. The sky darkened and, any minute, the thick wall of gray clouds would open and pour rain. The impending downpour and early fall evenings caused the streetlights to flicker on above him. He scrunched further into his jacket.

Rylee pushed open the door to the New Leaf Sewing Shop amidst a flurry of female voices and laughter. She stepped easily next to Bryan, and the two walked up the hill toward Maple Street. "I have great news for the cottages."

Her excited voice caught Bryan in the chest. He gazed at her with kindness and smiled. "Did you sell them?"

He moved Raisin away from her outstretched hand and continued to walk the dog by his side, making sure to walk on the outside of Rylee along the street side, protecting her from the occasional truck passing by. He enjoyed walking Raisin. The dog ambled comfortably next to him and seemed to enjoy him too. It was hard not to imagine what it would be like to have Raisin and Rylee in his life every day.

"No," Rylee said, playfully. "It's better. Cottage Magazine wants to feature the listing for an upcoming edition."

Bryan let out a whistle. "Colleen Sanders, right?"

"Right."

"Her brother runs the Beach and Sky Hotel," he said, grimacing. "No one much cares for how Shane runs his business, but he can pull the tourists in, so no one complains too much."

"Gracie and Katie weren't too fond of him."

"No." Bryan shook his head. "No one is too fond of him. Shane has the most rooms of any of the inns or hotels in the area. Most of the hotels are former boutique hotels, or hotels that were once one-story drive-by, ranch-style hotels. The Beach and Sky can easily offer deep discounts and beat out the others who can't offer the same specials."

"But how did he get such a large hotel?" Rylee asked. "I thought the beach hotels were under strict guidelines about their size." She angled her body slightly toward Bryan and stepped closer to him.

"It happened about seven years ago. "Bryan replied, trying hard not to lose his thoughts in the closeness of Rylee. "Jeremy Sanders bought a large stretch of land from Sawyer and built a huge high rise. No one knew exactly how the proposal passed City Council. There was a lot of speculation about timing. The council set the meeting for the permit to be two days before the holidays. Of course, no one was in town, and Jeremy loaded the rooms with his supporters. Colleen's brother, Shane, is part-owner and has run it for years."

"Colleen is part-owner now. She wants to hire me to redo the hotel, so it'd be more boutique and casual beach."

Bryan stopped short on the sidewalk. Rylee had been offered a job. A good job that would allow her to stay in Cranberry Bay. Excitement rose in his chest. He wanted to pump his hand in the air, swing her around, and kiss her. All his prayers had been answered. Rylee would stay, and he'd win the bet. The riverboat casinos would be his. The town would have a new means to attract tourists. He could see the lights shining in the empty buildings around him. New restaurants, coffee shops, and even a bookstore would fill what now lay dark and empty. He didn't dare hope, but he didn't want to think about what else Rylee staying would mean to him.

"Do you want me to take your grandmother's house off the market?" He couldn't keep the smile out of his voice.

"I don't know..." Rylee shook her head. "I think the cottage article is perfect. It will help us to sell them at a high price. Both our names will have good promotion. Yours as a good Realtor in the area, and mine as a decorator for future jobs on a national level. But..."

Bryan's hope flickered, and his heart dove back to his cold toes. "But?"

"But I'm not sure about taking the beach job, especially after what you just told me."

"It's a great job," he said, trying to remain optimistic yet not wanting to get his hopes dashed.

"It is," Rylee shook her head. "It may sound silly. But after a bad experience, I made a pact to myself to not take jobs that would harm mom-and-pop businesses. I can't always know about it, of course. But this seems like it would affect the other hotels nearby. If Colleen can discount all the rooms and undercut the other smaller businesses that would be similar to hers...well...it just feels wrong."

Even though Rylee's answer wasn't what he hoped for, Bryan's insides warmed. He stepped closer to her. Large drops of rain dropped out of the clouds, and, without thinking, Bryan linked his fingers with Rylee's. "Come on. I know a place we can go until the heavy rain passes over us."

Bryan guided her to a set of poorly lit stairs leading down to a small door with a sign, "Restorative Hardware."

The two stepped into the room, and Bryan's eyes adjusted to the dimly lit space filled with various pieces of old hardware and lighting fixtures. Rylee turned around in circles. "What is this place?"

"This," Bryan waved his right hand over the room, as if showing off a special home on a city history tour, "is the place where old hardware from our Cranberry Bay houses ends up. When people have a remodel and want to get rid of their old fixtures, Bill and his team save them. He resells the items on the Internet and gives the owner half of the profits."

"Just like Ivy's antique store," Rylee said, smiling. "I bet I've bought from him without realizing. I've purchased a lot of vintage hardware and lighting to add to some of the homes I've decorated."

She walked toward a faded green dresser and pulled open the top drawer. Her sharp gasp filled the room as she pulled out three light-blue-and-white seashell drawer knobs. All the worry dropped from her features. Her face filled with the round joy of a child in a toy shop.

"How long has the store been here? I don't remember it when I used to visit."

Bryan ran his finger over a bronze light stand. "Your Grandpa used to spend a lot of time in here. That's how I first met him. This shop was the first place I learned to fix things." Bryan leaned back against a tall wooden counter. He crossed one leg over the other. "I always felt accepted by your Grandpa. I struggled finding my place at home. Sawyer was always good at sports, and Dad expected me to be like him. But I couldn't ever seem to live up to his expectation."

"So you came here." Rylee finished for him. Time had given Bryan an emotional honesty she hadn't experienced with him in their younger days.

"Yes." Bryan smoothed the lampshade under his fingers. "Bill showed me how to fix things as they came in. I felt important when I was here. And then..." Bryan swallowed, remembering the day as it had happened, "my Dad died."

He had heard the sirens racing up the hill to their home. In his gut, he had known something was wrong. He'd ridden his bike as fast as he could up the hill, but by the time he got there, it was too late. A heart attack had taken Dad's life, altering the Shuster family forever.

Rylee didn't say anything, but her gentle eyes caressed him.

"After Dad died, I couldn't focus on anything. I spent a lot of time on my skateboard, running around town after dark, and getting into trouble. The police finally had enough and tossed me into juvenile detention. It wasn't a long stay, and then your grandfather stepped up."

"I didn't know that," Rylee said, and frowned. "I thought Grandpa was your mentor."

"He was," Bryan said quietly. "My court-appointed mentor."

"Why didn't you ever tell me?" Rylee stepped around the dresser. She stood next to Bryan and placed her hand on his forearm.

"Because," Bryan looked up at her as pain filled his chest, "it wasn't something I was proud of. I wanted you to be proud of me."

"It wouldn't have mattered," Rylee said, emotion clogging her voice. "I loved you." Her voice caught.

In her eyes, Bryan saw the truth. She still loved him, just as he still loved her.

Bryan stepped up beside Rylee and inhaled her sweet scent. He leaned down and his lips brushed her cheek. He ran his hand down her arm and picked up her hand. Gently, he threaded his fingers through hers.

"Why?" He whispered, his voice hoarse with sorrow. "Why did you walk away from us?"

"Because," Rylee said, her voice choked with tears. "I couldn't let you…"

A gust of wind caught the open door and slammed it against the side of the building.

She brushed a tear off her cheek and blinked. "Where is Raisin? He was right here."

"Raisin!" Bryan said.

Rylee dropped the seashell knobs to the concrete floor with a clatter and raced to the door. Bryan trailed after her and up the stairs, into the now raging rainstorm.

"Raisin!" Rylee called as a large truck whooshed past them on the road. "What if he's on the road somewhere? He'll be killed."

"He won't be." Bryan's heart pounded. It'd been his fault Raisin escaped. He'd gotten so caught up talking about his Dad, he'd dropped the leash. Raisin had walked out into the storm. Rain sliced across his cheeks, chilling him, and plastering his hair to his head.

"Start walking toward your grandmother's house. I'll take the lower road along Main Street. We'll find him."

"No wait." Rylee pointed to the curvy road leading up to her grandmother's house. "He's there."

Bryan grabbed Rylee's hand. "Come on."

The two jogged up the street. Their footsteps pounded on the pavement. Ahead of them, Lauren kneeled with Raisin. Her bike lay tossed on the ground beside her. She waved at Bryan.

"Look what I found! A dog!"

"Thank-you so much. That's my dog." Rylee grabbed Raisin's wet leash. She kneeled down and wrapped her arms around his wet fur and burrowed her face against his nuzzle. "He escaped from the Restorative Hardware shop."

Lauren's smile faded, and she ducked her head. Her wet curly hair dropped over her face. "I thought he was lost. I wanted to keep him. I've always wanted a dog."

"Come on." Bryan pointed to Lauren's yellow slicker, which hung unzipped around her bulky green fisherman's sweater. "Zip up your jacket. What are you doing out here in the rain anyway?"

"I had after-school clubs." Lauren wrinkled her nose. She jerked her zipper mid-way up her small body. "I hate after-school clubs."

"What was your after-school club?" Rylee asked, straightening. She wiped a long strand of wet hair away from her eyes.

"Games."

"You don't like games?" Bryan asked.

"I hate them." Tears pooled in Lauren's eyes. "I never win."

"Well," Bryan said, dropping his arm over Lauren's shoulder and pulling her close to him. "We will have to change that. We'll start practice right away. Tonight in fact."

"Can Raisin stay too?" Lauren gazed at him and her eyes filled with hope.

Bryan raised his right eyebrow and looked at Rylee. "We'd love to have an extra player."

A shadow crossed Rylee's face. "I don't know. I should get home. I want to see what happened in the backyard with the pipes."

"The pipes will still be there later," Bryan said, pleading with his eyes for her to stay. "Jim will have turned off the water anyway." He shifted his weight onto his left leg.

"Please." Lauren pressed up against Raisin. "I really like your dog." She cleared her throat. "And I bet I might really like you too."

Bryan chuckled. Lauren had Sawyer's way of charming everyone to get what she wanted.

"Well," Rylee gazed at Lauren, as a softness stretched across her face. "Okay. Just for a little while. But Raisin will need to dry off before he can be in your house."

"Not a problem," Bryan said, his voice light. "We have plenty of towels."

Behind them, a porch light turned on and the front door opened. Rebecca stood framed in the golden light. She wore a pair of black slacks and a cream sweater. Her gray hair encircled her round face.

"Lauren, please bring your bike under the porch. It's pouring."

"Coming Grandma!" Lauren rolled her bike up the walkway as Rylee, Bryan, and Raisin followed behind.

"What a mess the rain dragged in." Rebecca held open the door wide. "Come in. I'm just about to build a fire. Someone take this dog to the back porch and dry him off."

"I'll start the fire, Mom." Bryan leaned over and kissed his Mom on the cheek. "Why don't you sit down? Lauren can take care of Raisin."

"You know I can't sit down," Rebecca said, and smiled at Bryan. "I've got groceries in the car. I was planning to make a big pot of chili tonight." She turned to Rylee. "Rylee Harper. It's so good see you again. I'm so sorry about your grandmother."

"Thank you," Rylee said, her voice gentle.

"What happened to your grandmother?" Lauren danced in the door. She ignored Bryan's command to take Raisin to the backdoor. Raisin trailed after her and sat down. Water ran off his fur and onto the hardwood floors of the front entryway.

"She died." Rylee took the towel Bryan held out to her. She toweled Raisin dry. After Raisin was dry, she pulled off her boots and set them under the bench near the front door.

"My mother died." Lauren dropped to the ground and yanked off her shoes. She wiggled her toes inside her thick navy socks. "I miss her."

"I miss my grandmother too," Rylee replied.

Bryan padded in his socked feet to her. He placed his hand lightly on Rylee's back. He felt her tense and then relax against his touch.

"Lauren." Rebecca rubbed her granddaughter's hair through her forefinger and thumb. "Why don't you go into the kitchen? I've got brownies on the counter for you."

"Brownies!" Lauren hopped up and twirled down the hallway toward the kitchen. Raisin trailed after her.

Rebecca straightened. She placed her hand on her left knee as a flash of pain crossed her face.

"Mom?" Bryan leapt to her side.

"It's nothing," Rebecca said, tension etched in her voice. "Just the damp weather makes my knee hurt, I suppose."

"Have you seen a doctor?" Bryan asked.

Mom never liked doctors. She said all it took to heal was a little time and some rest. The only time Bryan had ever seen Mom go to a doctor was after Dad died. She hadn't been sleeping and finally broke down to ask for a prescription to help her sleep at night.

"I'm fine," Rebecca said. "Please don't worry about me. But maybe I will take you up on that offer to sit down right now. Can you and Rylee manage the groceries?"

"Of course."

Worry filled Bryan's chest. Sawyer had been right. Mom wasn't okay, and she was trying to hide her illness from them. In the morning, he'd sit down with her and convince her to make an appointment to see their longtime family doctor.

Ten minutes later, Bryan and Rylee had unloaded eight sacks of groceries onto the kitchen counter. Rebecca sat at the kitchen table and sipped a tall glass of ice water.

Bryan reached into the bags and pulled out cans of pumpkin. "What's all this? Thanksgiving isn't for another week."

"The store was having a special on Thanksgiving ingredients. It's my favorite holiday, and I can't wait to start baking pies." Rebecca peered out the kitchen window as rain lashed against the windowpanes. "I might start this evening. It's a good night to be at home. The flood warnings are up for the rivers. The library board canceled their monthly meeting. I hear the City Council isn't meeting tonight either."

Rebecca turned to Rylee. "Why don't you join us for Thanksgiving? If you don't have plans."

Bryan stepped up behind Rylee. He rubbed her lower back. "That's a great idea."

"Thank you," Rylee said, flushing. "I'd like that. I'll dig out my grandmother's recipes and see if I can find the bread she used to make."

Rebecca leaned against the counter. A grimace crossed her face.

"Why don't you rest tonight?" Bryan pulled out a large skillet and two cutting boards. He placed the wooden boards side-by-side. He grabbed two tomatoes and handed one to Rylee. She stepped up beside him and methodically cut into her tomatoes into small chunks. "If the flood warnings are up, Adam will be down from his cabin at the mountain park. Last time he stayed during floods, a mudslide caught him up there for three days."

"I haven't heard from him, yet." Rebecca peered out the window "He'll most likely stay until the last possible minute to make sure everything gets taken care of at the campgrounds. How's your Dad, Rylee?"

Rylee stiffened. "He's fine. Thank you."

"We would love to see him again in Cranberry Bay." Rebecca shook her head and smiled. "I had such a crush on him in high school. He was a few years older than me, and I thought the world of him. We all did. We all hoped he might come back to Cranberry Bay to visit. But he never did."

Rylee's mouth tightened. Her knife moved up and down as she sliced through the tomatoes, sending small spurts of juice spraying against the tiled back wall of the kitchen.

Bryan leaned closer to her. "Take it easy on those vegetables. No one is getting hurt here."

Rylee eased back on the knife, but she didn't smile. Her hands gripped the handle and turned white.

Before Bryan could say anything. Lauren flew into the kitchen from the mudroom. Raisin ran behind her.

"Did you know they're closing my elementary school?" She stuffed the brownie the rest of the way into her mouth. Crumbs dropped onto the kitchen floor, and Raisin gobbled them up.

"Not yet," Bryan said. Rumors in the small town flew easily and frequently. The last thing Lauren needed was more change. She'd had enough to deal with over the last two years with her mother dying.

"They told everyone today at a special assembly. Some of the teachers cried." Lauren balled her hands into fists and pumped the air. "We have to go to the beach school. The bus ride is over twenty minutes, and I get car sick." She clutched her stomach and stumbled around the kitchen.

"Why are they closing your school?" Rylee slid the cut tomatoes off the cutting board and into a silver bowl.

"There aren't enough kids in Cranberry Bay." Lauren sidled up to her. "I think you should move here and get married. I bet you have a lot of friends. You could encourage your friends to move here too. Everyone could have kids, and I could see Raisin every day."

Rylee flushed a deep red and turned to Bryan. "They're closing the elementary school?"

"It looks like it," Bryan said gruffly. "I hoped it wasn't true, and they were going to give it more time before a decision was made. The student population has dropped so much they don't have the tax dollars to run the school any more."

The room felt claustrophobic to Bryan. Everything closed in on him. Once the school closed, Cranberry Bay had no hope of recruiting families. He'd seen it happen up and down the small coastal towns. Without dairy farms or tourists to sustain them, the towns died. Now it would happen to Cranberry Bay. The town he loved was dying, and he wasn't going to be in time to save it.

Bryan dropped his sliced tomatoes into the bowl. It was time to approach the City Council about his plan. He had to move forward, even if the bet hadn't quite been won yet. If the town knew about the riverboats, then maybe it would give everyone hope, and they could hold on a little longer before closing the elementary school. It was his only chance to save the town and the people he cared about the most.

Chapter Eleven

Rylee wiped her hands on her full-length denim apron and surveyed the staged cottage. The freshly painted walls glowed creamy white in the lamplight. A couple of old apple carts were turned upside down and placed as nightstands next to the wrought-iron double bed. Blue glass jars filled with fake daisies sat on each nightstand and complimented the patchwork quilt tossed over the bottom of the bed. A white comforter lay across the bed, on top of which was a thick pillow. It was framed with an old painted door she'd used as a headboard. A pile of wood lay in the fireplace. A basket of marshmallows, graham crackers, and toasting sticks was arranged inside a metal bucket beside a white rocking chair with blue-striped cushions. Two white pillar candles rested on the wooden coffee table. A two-person denim loveseat sat against the wall. The room smelled of cinnamon from a glowing candle on the small kitchen counter.

At the round, two-person table, Maddie painted glass mason jars a light white. She wore a canvas apron splattered with paint splotches. Beside her sat a stack of red-and-white straws and a wooden tray. It'd been Maddie's idea to turn the mason jars into lemonade glasses, and Rylee couldn't help but agree. The painted glass added a nice touch to their last cottage. It was her favorite; it had been the one in which she'd once told Bryan how much she loved him.

At first, she'd been afraid of the memories that threatened to engulf her when she opened the door. But after two weeks of working on the other cottages, it'd become obvious she couldn't wait any longer to start staging the final one. And when she did open the door, she'd found the cottage stripped bare. The light-blue curtains she remembered were gone. The kitchen cabinets no longer held stray fishing gear or random coffee mugs with motivational fishing sayings that made her laugh. Instead, the cottage was a blank slate, something she dove into with gusto. She had wanted to capture the feeling she once had when she believed nothing could ever stand in the way of their love for each other.

Rylee grabbed a white bakery bag from the kitchen counter and pulled out an oatmeal raisin cookie. She broke it in half and placed one part on a napkin in front of Maddie. "Hungry?"

"This is so much fun." Maddie looked up at Rylee. Her eyes glowed. She waved her paintbrush in the air like a flag.

"You've been a big help," Rylee said, and smiled. "I honestly don't know how I could have done it without you."

Maddie's youthful ideas had brought an innocent charm to the cottages. A bright orange pillow picked up at a garage sale one Saturday, which Rylee was sure would never work anywhere, had fit easily into what they were calling the sunflower cottage. A playful pink flamingo statue was tucked into the top shelf of the kitchen of the first cottage, beside an assortment of pink water glasses for picnics. But Maddie's favorite find was an old croquet set, which she'd placed under the eaves of the end cottage closest to the fire pit.

Maddie's cell phone buzzed in her paisley bag, but she didn't move to answer it. She hadn't responded to any of the calls that had come in during the last hour. Rylee knew better than to pry. At the sewing circle, Lisa had confessed it'd been a struggle getting Maddie to attend school. She had finally enrolled Maddie in an online program and gave up fighting with her to go to school in Cranberry Bay. After recognizing Maddie's interest in the antique shop, Ivy had found a place for Maddie. She asked her to organize items and package things to mail out to online sales customers. In the hours Rylee and Maddie worked together, Maddie didn't talk about her friends, school, or life in Seattle. But she wasn't withdrawn and sullen either. She enjoyed chatting with Rylee about design work and asked a lot of thoughtful questions. Maddie usually stopped by Sasha's bakery and purchased a couple pastries, which she shared with Rylee before getting started on the day's activities.

Rylee had decided her most important job was to build Maddie's trust in her. She remembered all too well her own days of working and trying to hide her Dad's gambling addiction from prying adults who wanted to know too much about her. Her grandparents' home was the only place she felt nurtured and cherished, without someone feeling sorry for her or having to explain her father's problems. She wanted to give the same to Maddie.

Rylee walked to the window and gazed down on the rushing river. "Maddie. Does the river seem like it has risen?"

Maddie stuck her brush into a can of water and walked to the window that overlooked a small wooden porch above the river. "I can't tell. But I'm sure if it was going to flood, Bryan would have sandbags."

"Mmmm…" Rylee nodded absently as two pairs of headlights flashed across the cottage windows and cast shadows along the walls.

In minutes, Bryan strode through the door. His presence filled the small room as water ran off his coat and onto the red doormat. Rylee's heart leaped, the way it always did every time she saw him.

"Maddie," he said sharply. "Lisa and Sawyer have been calling your cell phone for hours. Why didn't you answer?"

Maddie shrugged. "I didn't hear it."

Rylee frowned. They'd both heard her cell phone.

"Go on before you get in any more trouble." Bryan waved at the door. "Lisa is waiting for you in the car. The road to Sawyer's will be washed out if the rain keeps up."

Maddie hopped from the table. She stepped to the small sink and ran her paintbrush underneath a slow trickle of water.

"Is the water pressure low in here?" Bryan strode to the sink. He reached around Maddie and turned up the faucet. The water flowed freely.

Maddie maneuvered herself away from Bryan. "I liked it that way," she mumbled.

Rylee's heart ached for both Maddie and Bryan. She heard the way Maddie talked about the things she used to do with her family in Cranberry Bay, and Rylee saw her strong need and desire to somehow be a part of her family again. Rylee also knew it could be hard to connect with teenagers sometimes. But she hoped the two of them would at least find a way back to the special bond they'd once shared.

"See you tomorrow?" Maddie laid her paintbrush on a paper towel and walked over to her colorful, floral bag. It'd been an antique shop find a few weeks ago.

Katie had worked with her to sew on a new strap. Maddie hefted the bag onto her shoulders.

"We should have everything finalized tomorrow. I want to do a final run-through of each cottage and make sure we didn't forget something." Rylee consulted her yellow tablet with the scratched off list. "But it looks like we're done after tomorrow. Your painted jars are the last thing to put in place." She smiled at Maddie. She hoped the girl felt reassured by the job she had done.

"Okay." Maddie's face fell as she pulled on her long, black coat. "I guess I'll see you around."

"Thank you. Great job today."

Maddie gave Rylee a small smile. She ducked her head and slipped outside into the early evening darkness.

Bryan shut the door behind Maddie and faced Rylee. He leaned against the wall and his blue eyes glowed intently at her. Her face flushed. She had tried not to think about his kiss, but it seemed to be the only thing filling her waking hours.

Rylee picked up the tray for the glass jars. She set it on the counter and returned to the table, standing by a chair to steady herself.

Bryan walked behind her and set his hands lightly on her shoulder. He massaged her neck, and his fingers smoothed away her tension. Trying hard not to groan, Rylee surrendered to his touch. Rain pounded on the roof and against the windows. The candle glowed on the table.

"Bryan..." Rylee's voice sounded hoarse to her, and her knees felt weak. She grasped the back of the chair as Bryan's hands continued to do a dance alongside her neck.

"Cold?" Bryan whispered against her neck. "I can start a fire. Someone has set out logs for us."

"Mmmm…" Rylee breathed as she closed her eyes and leaned back into Bryan's arms. "A fire would be great. The matches are in the kitchen. Top drawer."

"Got it."

Rylee walked to the couch and sank down against the blue-and-white striped pillows. Raisin, sleeping on a thick dog bed she had made for him at the last sewing circle, let out a small yip. Her heart pounded as she tucked her legs underneath her and settled back on the couch. When Bryan touched her, she felt herself sing with the pleasure of coming home to a place she only found with him, a place she wanted to last forever. And maybe, she thought, maybe it was possible to stay in this place forever. She loved being a part of the women's sewing circle and making plans for the holiday vintage market. She enjoyed spending time in Bryan's kitchen with his Mom and niece, Lauren. It reminded her of being with Grandma and Grandpa. Maybe she could trust Dad had kicked his gambling habit this time and didn't need her. Maybe.

Bryan kneeled on the floor in front of the fireplace. He carefully tucked newspaper and a few pieces of kindling under the logs and lit a match. The fire smoked, and, as the paper caught, the small sticks smoldered under the heat.

"I think that'll do it." He leaned back on his heels. "It should be warm in here in no time."

Rylee smiled at him as he settled himself on the couch beside her and picked up her hand. He threaded their fingers together and caressed the inside of her wrist with his thumb. She shivered with his touch.

The fire outlined his profile and turning, Rylee ran her hand alongside his face. "Bryan," she breathed.

Bryan shifted and gathered her in his arms. He lowered his mouth to hers, and she surrendered to the kiss.

* * *

"My Dad used to say his favorite part of a storm was a cozy fire." Rylee curled deeper into Bryan's arms. "We don't get very many stormy days in Vegas. But when it rains, he always liked to build a fire and read his paper."

"Where is your Dad, Rylee?" Bryan thumbed circles on her lower arm and smoothed a strand of hair from her forehead. Rylee had never talked much about her Dad. He assumed she tired of talking about his baseball days.

Rylee stared straight into the fire. "He lives in Vegas." Her voice sounded strangled and cold.

"Rylee?" Bryan touched her arm.

Rylee stood and walked to the window overlooking the river. She crossed her arms, as if trying to hold it all inside, and said, "Dad is not who everyone believes him to be. He has a gambling addiction. He has struggled with it since I was a child."

Raisin shook himself and ambled over to her. He leaned his nose against her leg. She reached down and stroked his back.

Bryan stepped up beside her. "Is that why he never comes back home?" Bryan wanted to gather Rylee into his arms and hold her. He wanted to tell her Dad's history didn't matter. What mattered was the love that existed between them.

"Dad spent all the money he made playing his one season in baseball on gambling. Mom supported him until she died. Then I picked up what I could. Grandma and Grandpa sent money sometimes. They tried to keep it from everyone in town. They knew people would be disappointed if they found out what had really happened to their hero."

"Is that why you never returned to Cranberry Bay?"

Rylee turned around to face Bryan, anguish in her eyes. "The morning after you proposed, I got a call from the Las Vegas Police Department. They'd arrested Dad for fighting. He didn't have anyone to bail him out. When I got there, he promised he'd stop gambling. He said he just needed to get back on his feet. I believed him, and I believed I was going to come back to Cranberry Bay."

"But he didn't get back on his feet?"

"No," Rylee said, her voice choked with sobs. "He didn't. At first, everything was fine. I even made reservations for plane tickets to return for the holidays. At Thanksgiving, he started gambling again. After that, it was always the same. He'd win big and promise never to return to the tables. Then a few days later, he'd lose it all and end up sleeping on my couch."

"And your grandmother gave you the house but not him."

"After I inherited the house, I felt terrible. Dad wouldn't talk to me for weeks. He was so angry. I promised Dad we'd share the proceeds, and I'd buy us a place in San Diego. I hoped he would get away from gambling." She bent her head and studied the floor.

"You can't stop his gambling, Rylee." Bryan placed his arms around her and pulled her close. "It's not your fault he has an addiction. You can't change that addiction. Only he can change it."

"I know." Tears streamed down Rylee's face. "But he's the only family I have left. I can't just leave him.

He needs me. What will he do without me? Live on the street?"

Rylee slipped out of Bryan's arms. She pulled on her jacket and called Raisin to her side. Quickly, she opened the door and stepped into the rainy night.

Anguished, Bryan tossed a small bucket of water onto the dying flames in the fireplace. She'd trusted him enough to tell him why she couldn't stay in Cranberry Bay, but it didn't change anything. Rylee believed her Dad needed her. She believed she could save her Dad from himself. She would leave again, taking his heart with her, and there was nothing he could do to stop her.

Rylee's scream cut through the silent night. He raced to the door and threw it open to find the river overflowing its banks.

Chapter Twelve

Rylee lifted one wet foot from the pool of water. Her car tires were submerged in at least a foot of water that had risen to within a few feet of the cottage. She hadn't meant to scream, but she'd been so surprised to find herself wading in the thick and muddy river water, she couldn't help it.

"Rylee!" Bryan stood in the lit doorframe. "Don't move. I'll be right there." His deep voice boomed across the courtyard.

"I'm fine." Rylee spoke above the rain, which poured down in buckets. "But my car is flooded."

Bryan slipped back into the cottage, and Rylee stared at the muddy water covering the courtyard. The croquet set floated beside the barbecue. The flowerpots floated beside the picnic table. It would take days to bring the gravel paths and grassy yard back to where the cottages could be shown with some confidence of attracting a buyer. Rylee wiped rain away from her eyes. At the rate of this storm, it looked like the river hadn't even begun its damage yet.

Bryan splashed across the flooded yard. "We'll take my truck. The wheels sit higher than your car." He held out his hand to her. She easily slipped hers into his warm one.

He squeezed her palm. "Ready?"

Rylee nodded. She held onto Raisin's leash and guided the dog to Ryan's truck. He stepped beside her and unlocked the passenger-side door.

Bryan looked into her eyes. "I'm glad we were together for the storm."

Rylee's heart turned over as she gazed into his blue eyes. She reached up and ran her hand along his cheek. "I am too."

Bryan took her hand from his cheek. He wrapped his fingers with hers and placed them both next to his heart. For a minute, neither of them said a word.

Raisin nosed his body in between the two of them, and Rylee pulled away.

Bryan turned and unlocked the backdoor. Raisin jumped into the backseat while Rylee slipped into the passenger side. She reached over to unlock Bryan's door. Bryan slipped into the driver's side and reached into the middle console to pull out his cell phone. "I'll get a couple people to help sandbag. The river hasn't flooded like this in over two decades."

"I'll help you." Rylee reached into her bag for her cell phone. She scrolled through the numbers until she found Ivy's home number.

In minutes, both Rylee and Bryan had secured a handful of people to help with the sandbags. Ivy promised to call Sasha, Gracie, and Katie, while Cole pledged to pick up Mitch and Josh on his way to pick up the sandbags at City Hall. Bryan turned on his windshield wipers and pulled his truck out of the gravel lot. He turned toward the buildings on Main Street.

"Cole will have the back of City Hall opened. He was working late tonight and said he'd been watching the river levels all day. I'll check on the flood stage with him, but the cottages should be okay as long as we can get them sandbagged tonight."

Rylee bit her lower lip as Bryan's tires squealed on the pavement, and he made a sharp right into the back parking lot of a small brick building. A black SUV was parked alongside the building. A tall man hefted sandbags into the back.

"Cole!" Bryan turned off his ignition, opened the door, and stepped out into the rain.

Rylee slipped out of her seatbelt and followed Bryan. She vaguely remembered Cole as one of the boys Bryan hung out with as a teen. Now a tall, full-fledged man, he wore jeans and a dark rain jacket with a blue baseball cap. Cole greeted her and continued his work.

A small red four-door car pulled in behind the black SUV, and Sasha hoped out. "I came as soon as I could." Her curly hair bounced in a ponytail on top of her head. She stepped over and embraced Rylee in a large hug. "Don't worry. It'll all work out."

Rylee swallowed the lump in her throat at Sasha's warmth. "Thanks."

"I've grabbed a tray of cookies from the bakery. We're going to need sustenance for this job, and I've got a whole set of colorful cut-out turkeys that are just begging to be eaten. Tyler helped me frost them. I thought he did a really good job, and I might have some competition for my job someday."

"But those are for Thanksgiving." Rylee protested.

Sasha shrugged and smiled at her. "I don't think we'll be very busy with this kind of storm. I'd rather give everyone a treat now than let them go to waste."

"Where is Tyler?" Rylee looked around for Sasha's eight-year-old son.

"He's with my sister." Sasha's voice darkened. "Her family always rents a large house at the beach for the holidays. He wanted to spend the night with his cousins. It's not something I can ever give him, and I try to let it bother me. But," she swallowed, "sometimes it does."

Rylee reached out to hug Sasha. "I bet he loves it. You're a good Mom." For a minute her heart constricted. Would she ever get to experience the love of being a mother like Sasha?

"Come on," Sasha said gruffly. "Let's get these cars and trucks loaded up with the sandbags. The guys don't get all the fun around here."

Ten minutes later, all three cars were loaded with sandbags, and they made a caravan down Main Street toward the cottages. Three more cars parked up the hill from the cottages waited in the dark night. Bryan's headlights swept across the water-filled parking lot and yard.

"Everyone came to help. I didn't expect..." The words died in Rylee's throat.

Bryan reached over and palmed her thigh. "This is how we work in Cranberry Bay. We all pitch in."

Rylee nodded. She was afraid if she said anything the tears would start. It was what she'd always heard from her grandparents about the storms in the small town: Stories of residents banding together to overcome days without power in high windstorms. Stories of how everyone pitched in to help with meals, food, and childcare. It wasn't the same as when the power went out in Vegas due to a loss in the grid system. She always huddled in the dark, by herself, hoping that the emergency battery to the security system in her condo had kicked in. In Cranberry Bay, everyone showed up to help out.

Rylee slipped out of the truck as Katie stepped toward her. She placed a blue blanket around her shoulders. "Are you okay?"

"Yes." Rylee fingered the blanket around her shoulders. "This is one of your quilts from the shop."

Katie looked into her eyes and smiled. "It's okay. What better way to use a quilt than to help out a good friend? I'm sorry this is the way your romantic evening ended."

"How did you know?" Rylee asked, wide-eyed and surprised at Katie's words.

"How did I not know?" Katie said, the smile evident in her voice. "The two of you have been grinning like teenagers every time you are around each other. Your secret is safe with me, unless..." she paused, "the two of you don't want it to be."

"I don't know how to feel right now," Rylee said. "There are things I have to work out."

"I'm sure you can work it out," Ivy said as she stepped up beside them. She clapped her gloved hands together and nodded toward Bryan. "I've never seen him as happy as he's been the last few weeks. He can't stop talking about you."

Rylee flushed at the compliment.

"Grab a sandbag." Cole stood on the bed of Bryan's truck. "We've got work to do."

The women set up a line and passed the sandbags to each other until a small, stacked row lay beside every cottage and along the riverside.

"That should hold it." Josh wiped his forehead. He peered down the street to the pub. "I hope they've got their sandbags out. They'll be flooded just like the cottages."

"Wait a minute." Sasha ducked into her car and called over her shoulder. "I've got something for everyone." She returned quickly and passed out the colorful decorated turkey cookies. "It won't hold you for long, but it's the best I could do at such a short notice."

"These are great," Josh said, biting off the head of one of the sugar cookies. "Great icing."

"That's Tyler's work," Sasha said, her voice echoed with pride. "This was his first job. He'll be disappointed customers didn't buy them."

"He's a good kid," Josh said. He swallowed the last of his cookie and wiped his hands on his dark-blue jeans. "I'm sorry Greg didn't stick around."

Startled at the mention of Tyler's Dad, Rylee turned to face Sasha. She had never talked about the father of her son in the sewing circle.

Sasha shifted away from Josh and crumpled a bakery bag. "I better get back. I'm whipping up the pies for my sister's celebration tomorrow at her beach place."

In a flurry of good-byes and hugs, Sasha said her goodnights and hopped into her car and pulled out of her space.

"You know not to talk about Greg." Katie frowned at Josh after Sasha's car pulled away. "And right before the holidays too."

"Sorry," Josh said. "I just feel so bad every time I see that kid without his Dad. It didn't have to be this way."

For a minute, Rylee wondered if Josh had feelings for Sasha and that was why he never noticed Ivy.

"Come on." Katie grabbed napkins from the group clustered around the truck. "I'll give you a ride home, Rylee. It's on my way."

"I'm giving her a ride." Bryan stepped up beside her. He dropped his arm over her shoulder and squeezed. "Raisin is in the car waiting." He nodded toward his truck where Raisin peered out the window at them with his nose pressed against the glass.

"Okay." Katie hugged her. "But call us and let us know if you need anything." She placed her hands on her hips. "I hope this is the last of it, and nothing happens to those cottages before Colleen can write her article."

Colleen. In the middle of her evening with Bryan and with the flooding, Rylee had forgotten the interview Colleen was doing with her the day after Thanksgiving. She looked around the dark yard. It'd be a muddy mess for the pictures. Her shoulders tensed. She thought of how everything would look in the daylight. Mud on every surface, pools of water, and the stench of the river everywhere. There wasn't time to get everything cleaned up.

"Don't worry." Bryan drew her closer. "She can take pictures of all the work you did inside the cottage. That's what counts."

"I hope you're right." Rylee bit down on her lower lip sharply.

"Let me get you home." Bryan opened the passenger door. Drops of water dripped from Bryan's broad shoulders, and he shivered. Rylee leaned over and wiped water from his right arm. Her fingers trailed down to his forearms. She removed the blanket from around her body and placed it over his shoulders. "You're freezing."

Bryan reached out and picked up her hand. He squeezed lightly and smiled at her. "It's okay," he said, still smiling. "Nothing a good hot shower won't cure."

Rain pounded on the roof, and Bryan placed his key into the ignition. "We better get out of here before the storm gets worse." He glanced in the rearview mirror and backed the car up.

In minutes, they pulled up in front of Rylee's dark home. Rylee shifted to face him. She wanted to say something about the way she'd left the cottage earlier in the evening. "Bryan I…"

"It's okay." Bryan leaned over and placed a kiss on her lips. "It's been a long night. We don't have to talk about this now. You're still coming to Mom's for Thanksgiving tomorrow afternoon?"

"Yes," Rylee said, looking up at him. "I'm looking forward to it."

"Good." Bryan kissed her again. His lips soft with tenderness. "I'll see you tomorrow."

Chapter Thirteen

Rylee entered the dark living room and walked to the hall table. She flicked on the stained-glass table lamp. It'd been a wedding anniversary gift. That summer, Grandma insisted she didn't need anything. But Grandpa wouldn't let a moment pass to declare his love for Grandma. Grandpa had asked Rylee to join him on a trip over the mountains to Portland. Rylee enjoyed combing the shops with Grandpa, and both had known the stained-glass lamp was perfect, for Grandma loved all things glass. Grandma had cried when she opened the gift and promised to always leave the light on as a visual display of their everlasting love. Rylee had kept the tradition going and loved seeing the glowing lamp. The light reminded her of the love between her grandparents and of their ever-present spirit.

Rylee followed Raisin into the kitchen. She filled his bowl with a cup of dry food and placed it before him. As Raisin gulped his food, she opened a kitchen cabinet and pulled out Grandma's old cookbooks. She had planned to donate them to the local library book sale, but hadn't found the heart to do so yet. Now she flipped open the yellowed and fragile pages. She smiled at her grandmother's familiar handwriting. Grandma's notes marked a variation in ingredients or she had scrawled, "Good recipe," in the margins. Rylee's heart warmed. It was as if Grandma sat with her and instructed her.

Rylee flipped to a section with breads and slowly scanned recipes. She searched for her grandmother's pumpkin bread. Her grandmother had made the best pumpkin bread. Every year, she packaged a loaf and mailed it to Rylee. Rylee loved receiving those loaves a day or two before Thanksgiving. She often brought the bread to the office to share.

Rylee studied the recipe. It was listed as a quick bread and didn't seem too hard. A couple of cans of pumpkin, spices, flour, sugar, and eggs. She pulled a small, white tablet of paper from a basket of pens and other odd jumbled items and jotted down ingredients. Afterward, she checked the canisters sitting on the counter for flour and sugar. At the same time, a shadow passed outside the backdoor window.

"Raisin," Rylee hissed. "Raisin." Her heart pounded, and she held very still.

The dog growled low in his throat. Rylee reached in the drawer for a cutting knife. She placed it in front of her.

Raisin continued to growl as the person stepped onto the back steps and peered in the window. Rylee cursed herself for not pulling the curtains.

A knock on the door, and her Dad shouted, "Rylee!"

Rylee dropped the knife onto the counter. She grabbed hold of Raisin's collar, so he wouldn't fly out the door. "Good boy," she said. "But we know him."

Rylee stepped to the backdoor, twisted the deadbolt lock, and pulled open the door. "Dad."

Her father stood before her. Water dripped off his thin shoulders and balding head. A gutter overflowed and splashed water onto his T-shirt. Rylee sighed and grabbed Dad's arm. She pulled him away from the sputtering and splattering downspout. The gutter was one more thing to add to the house repairs. "What are you doing here?"

Dad stepped into the kitchen. He yanked off his wet coat. Water pooled on the floor beneath him as he dropped his black duffle bag and a small, over-the-shoulder case. "Transportation never was easy out to Cranberry Bay at this time of the year. I should have remembered the late November storms."

"But what are you doing here?" Rylee's pulse raced. She hadn't believed Dad when he said he would visit Cranberry Bay. He never had returned before. It had to be the sale of Grandma's house that pulled him here. She opened a top cabinet and pulled out a ceramic mug with the letters Cranberry Bay Festival stenciled in white. Her feelings engulfed her, and tears strangled her throat. She loved Dad, and nothing made her happier than being around him. But a part of her always tensed. She waited for the bad news. Dad always had bad news. Over the years, she'd gotten better at reading his moods. She knew when he'd won big and when he'd lost big. But he could still throw her off-guard. Rylee leaned against the counter and studied him. Which one would it be this time?

"I'm spending Thanksgiving with you." Dad wiped his forehead. He reached into his bag and pulled out a small tablet. "I told you I wanted to spend the holidays with you. The bus was supposed to be here this morning, but a landslide cut off the road. We had to detour all the way down to Seashore Cove and back. Took a heck of a long time to get out here." He looked at the open cookbooks on the counter. "Planning Thanksgiving dinner? If you make up a list of ingredients, I'll pop up to the store tomorrow and pick everything up for us."

"I just need to get a few things for the bread. I can do that." She wasn't going to tell him her dinner plans included the Shuster family home.

Dad rubbed his chin. "I wonder if the annual football game with the high school alumni still takes place up at the park. I'll swing by there tomorrow. It'll be great to see everyone."

Rylee stared at her Dad in amazement. He hadn't been back to Cranberry Bay in over four decades. His entire life had changed since he left with a celebration parade and town party. Grandma always kept Dad's baseball pictures in a photo album. She left it on the coffee table. Rylee had enjoyed thumbing through the pictures and seeing Dad, the town hero. So many residents of the small town had pinned their hopes on him. He was the son, the grandson, and the nephew everyone always wanted. No one but Rylee and her grandparents knew what had happened to that small-town boy. Grandma said it was the death of Rylee's mother that kick-started the gambling. Dad had been so devastated over losing his beloved wife, he turned to gambling as a way to cope. But Rylee knew better. She knew the gambling started long before her mother died. She'd lay awake listening to her parents fighting. She'd packed her bags in the middle of the night to escape from the men in dark suits who seemed to follow them. Her summers in Cranberry Bay were a welcome relief from the fear she lived with on a regular basis, and, like Grandma, she kept the secret. She didn't want to do anything to encourage Dad to show up and bring with him all the fear she felt in Vegas.

"Things aren't the same in Cranberry Bay." Rylee tried to discourage Dad from seeking out the town's annual football game with high school alumni. "I'm not sure they even host that game any more. They're closing the elementary school. People have left Cranberry Bay."

Dad loved a party. He loved an audience. If he knew Cranberry Bay was dying, he would not want to stay.

Anger constricted Rylee's chest. How dare Dad show up now? He severed all ties years ago. Dad scorned the small town. He said it was the last place he wanted to be. When she was little, a man and woman came to see them. Dad put the couple up in an expensive hotel and took the man out to play golf while Mom sat by the pool with the lady. Dad said it was his old high school buddy, and he wanted to show him a good time. But after the couple left, Dad closed the door and rolled his eyes. He said he never wanted to see anyone from Cranberry Bay again, and he'd promptly headed for the casinos.

"Of course people left Cranberry Bay." Dad shook his head. "It can't be helped in small towns like this one. The town stops growing when residents resist every change. The next thing you know, the town is a ghost town."

"You don't care about the town." Rylee leaned back against the counter. She crossed her hands over her chest. Her insides shook as she thought of the people she'd come to know in Cranberry Bay who called it home. Ivy and her passion for her antique shop. Katie, who carried on her Mom's store with her own vision. Sasha and her determination to raise her son on her own.

Dad studied Rylee. "Not really. I grew up here, but I made a life somewhere else. Things change. The faster you learn that, the better you'll be. It's good not to hold onto anything for too long."

Rylee shook her head. It wasn't just her sewing circle friends and Bryan who loved Cranberry Bay. She

146

loved Cranberry Bay for all the comfort and security she'd found in it over the years. She loved it for the way people helped each other and genuinely cared. The sandbag party to save the cottages. Bryan stopping at the side of the road. Rebecca Shuster opening her home to Rylee for the holidays.

Dad reached into his bag and pulled out a small laptop computer. He set it on the counter and powered it up. "You got wireless in here?"

"Yes." Rylee spit the words out through gritted teeth. "It's an open connection. There's no need for a password."

"Is that safe?" Dad slipped on a pair of reading glasses. He gazed at her over the steel frames.

"It's Cranberry Bay," Rylee said. "Things are safe here." She left out how scared she'd been to find Dad on the back porch.

"Crime happens in Cranberry Bay, too. You'd be wise to remember that." Dad turned back to his computer screen. She tried to stop herself from leaning over to see what Dad was doing. Was he looking at a bank statement? Or gambling online?

"I know what you're thinking." Dad looked up at her, and his eyes bored into hers. "But I've kicked the habit. No more gambling."

"No more gambling?" Hope rose in Rylee's chest and then crashed. Dad had promised to stop gambling in the past. But each time he returned to it within weeks. The last time was over a year ago. After a particularly bad loss, and the repossession of his car, he showed up on Rylee's doorstep. That night, Dad swore he was done with all gambling. There would be no more, but if she could loan him $5,000 dollars to pay off the last of his debts, he'd walk away a free and clear man and pay her back as soon as he could secure a stable job.

Too afraid that if she didn't, Dad would return to gambling, Rylee agreed to Dad's terms. She had just deposited a large check from a design project and easily wrote the check to Dad. She asked Dad if anyone was after him for money, and he denied it. Rylee hoped he told the truth. The last time he'd been in debt had been especially bad, and he'd been beaten to within seconds of ending his life. Dad spent over a month in the hospital and another three months in physical rehab. Even now, Rylee was never sure Dad had completely regained the use of his left shoulder.

"No more gambling." Dad glanced back at his computer screen and smiled.

"What are you doing?" Rylee asked, curious to see what brought one of his unexpected smiles to his face.

"Nothing," Dad moved to flip closed his computer, but not before Rylee saw the logo of an online dating site flash across the screen.

"You're using one of those online dating sites!" she cried, her voice filled with awe and surprise.

Dad's neck flushed. He looked up at her, and his eyes sparkled. "I thought it was time. I'm not getting any younger. I'd like to have someone to enjoy the remaining years I have left."

Rylee's heart contracted at her Dad's honest sentiment. Of course he would want a partner, just like she wanted to spend her life with someone she loved. Her mother had been gone for years, and Dad had never really dated. Although there were always single moms in her school classes, he never looked twice at them. "I'm too busy raising my daughter," he'd say. Only Rylee knew the truth; he was too busy spending evenings at the casinos, and his first love had always been gambling.

"You really are serious about stopping gambling," Rylee said.

"Yes," Dad said. "I am." He chuckled lightly. "Now how about you? There was that boy you once loved in Cranberry Bay, right? Is he still here?"

Rylee flushed from the roots of her hair down through her toes. She quickly turned away and busied herself with washing a glass in the sink.

"Rylee," Dad said, his tone light and teasing. "What's going on?"

"Nothing," Rylee said quickly. She turned around to face Dad. But she couldn't remove the smile from her lips.

"It doesn't look like nothing," Dad said. "Do I need to buy a tux for a wedding?"

"Oh," Rylee gasped. The thought of marrying Bryan filled her with a joy she hadn't dared feel. "I don't think so. I mean not yet..." But hope danced around the edges of her mind. If Dad had really kicked the habit, then he wouldn't need her to support him any more. She would be free to start her own life in Cranberry Bay. No one in Cranberry Bay would ever have to know about his past. He'd be a different man without gambling.

"I'm happy for you." Dad stood and embraced her. "You've worked really hard, and I know it hasn't been easy trying to support me over the years. I appreciate all that you've done for me. Now it's my turn to make it up to you. What do you say I move in here?"

"Here?" Rylee gasped. She looked around the kitchen. "To Grandma's house?"

"Yes," Dad said. "It's completely paid off. I've got money that I put into some investments, and I can help pay the expenses."

Rylee narrowed her eyes. "What type of investments, Dad?"

"Investments," Dad said. "Good investments." His firm tone told her the discussion was over. "If I move in with you. I can pick up the expenses. I know jobs aren't easy to find in this area, so that will give you some time to explore a bit."

Rylee stared at her Dad. She wanted to believe in Dad. If Dad really did have good investments, then he could carry the house expenses. She would have the freedom and time to set up her own business again. Once she did the work for Colleen, her name would get out. There were plenty of hotels in the surrounding beach towns that could use her services, not to mention owners of second-homes, when the market recovered. And she wouldn't have to sell her grandparents' beloved home.

"So." Dad said. "What are the Thanksgiving plans?"

"The Shuster family has invited me for dinner." Rylee straightened and smiled into Dad's eyes. "Why don't I call and ask if there is room for you?"

"I would love that," Dad said. "Rebecca Shuster was in school about the same time as me. She raised quite a family, I hear." He winked at her. "Including Bryan Shuster."

"Yes," Rylee said, as the heat moved through her again.

"Why don't you let me make that call in the morning?" He nodded toward the old rotary phone on the wall. "Does that thing work?"

"Yes. The old phone still works." Rylee said, a sudden giddiness filling her. Everything was going to work out. Dad had stopped gambling. He could return to the town again. And she and Bryan could finally be together again.

Chapter Fourteen

On Thanksgiving, Bryan woke to the smells of apple pie and cinnamon. The phone rang in the kitchen below his bedroom. His Mom's footsteps strode across the hardwood kitchen floor. Her cheery voice traveled through the air ducts into his room. Bryan stretched and smiled. Was it Sawyer calling to ask about the green-bean casserole he and Lauren always made together? Or maybe Adam calling to tell Mom he'd be late because he forgot to pick up the cranberries for his salad. Holidays at the Shuster house were always filled with laughter and good cheer. Bryan pushed back the covers and headed toward the bathroom. In a few hours, Rylee would join with them in their family celebration, and he couldn't wait to see her.

In the bathroom, Bryan flicked on the light. He had shared this bathroom with Sawyer and Adam. They had many fights for mirror-time during high school. But they never complained to Lisa, who had her own bathroom. As the only girl in the family, it seemed only right that Lisa had her privacy as a teen. The only sister of three brothers, she survived football games in the backyard, toy trucks scattered all over the living room, and dinner table talk that could easily break into burps and belches before Mom silenced everyone with one of her looks.

Bryan turned on the shower and stepped into the bathtub. He pulled the shower curtain closed. The hot water rained down on his face. It was useless to deny how he felt about Rylee. His attempt at not falling in love had failed miserably. She'd always been the only girl who could turn his heart to jelly and make him want to go to the ends of the Earth to protect her. As a woman, she had become even more attractive. There was a depth to her eyes that could only have been created by life experience and made him love her more as a woman than he had a girl.

She had captured his heart again. But his conscience nagged at him. What if it got out that he'd been involved in a bet to convince her to stay? How would Rylee feel knowing she was the object of that bet? At the time, it'd seemed like the best way to obtain the money he needed for the riverboat casinos. But now he doubted his decision. He didn't want to hurt Rylee, and if she found out she'd been used as a pawn, she'd be devastated.

Bryan turned off the water and stepped out of the shower. He grabbed a thick towel and wiped himself dry. If the cottages sold for a good price, he wouldn't need the bet. He could ask for corporate sponsors for the remaining monies for the riverboats. But would the cottages sell for a strong asking price? And was there enough time to sell them? Plus, the City Council still had to approve the riverboats, and without Sawyer's backing, how likely were the council members to approve something like the riverboat casinos? Everyone knew Sawyer was good for his word. He'd shown the town over and over that when he said he'd do something, he would do it. With Sawyer funding the riverboats, the community would know there was a good, strong intent behind the plan. But without that funding and Sawyer's seal of approval, Bryan doubted the City Council would approve his vision.

Bryan wrapped the towel around his waist and opened the mirror cabinet above the sink. The shelves looked as if none of the Shuster boys had ever left. Shaving creams, lotions, and razors, along with the yearly toothbrushes they always received from their annual dentist check-ups, filled the glass shelves his father had installed years ago. Bryan pulled out a can of shaving cream and sprayed a clump onto his palm. He lathered his face and stared at himself in the mirror.

He didn't have the same track record as Sawyer with the townspeople. They'd watched him take far too many risks and not come out the other side. He frowned as he remembered the time he wanted a skate park and tried to work with the parks department. The night the project was to be presented to City Council, he'd been caught in Portland with a friend who needed to move out of his house as soon as possible due to some late rental payments. Bryan missed the City Council meeting. Without his presentation, the City Council defeated the park. To the town, he was still a non-committed twenty-something aimlessly playing guitar in the beach pubs.

Bryan finished getting ready in the bathroom and padded into the bedroom. He pulled on a pair of dark jeans, a white T-shirt, and a green sweater and headed downstairs to the kitchen. His stomach growled at the sight of three apple and pumpkin pies sitting on the counter. A turkey roasted in the oven and filled the kitchen with the rich deep aroma he remembered so well from previous holidays. Rebecca took another sip of her coffee. She sat at the round kitchen table. A stack of cloth napkins, unfolded, lay beside her, along with napkin rings and small paper turkeys Lauren had made in school. Across the middle of each paper turkey, the names of family members were written in Lauren's newly learned cursive handwriting.

"Happy Thanksgiving." Bryan stepped over to the table. He gave his Mom a light kiss on the cheek.

She smiled at him. "Good morning. Did the phone wake you?"

Bryan shook his head, turned, and opened the refrigerator. He pulled out a carton of orange juice and reached for a glass in the upper kitchen cabinet. "I should have been up about an hour ago to help you. I'm sorry." The juice splashed onto the counter as he poured. He grabbed a towel and wiped the spot clean.

"No." Rebecca waved her hand toward Bryan. Her pink polished nails shone in the kitchen light. "It's good to see you resting. I know you've been working very hard on those cottages as well as trying to get your business up and running. An extra hour of sleep is good for you."

"What time is everyone coming?" Bryan took a big swig of his juice and swallowed. "Do you want me to set the table?" He pointed to the napkins, rings, and paper turkeys. "Lauren has created a masterpiece again." He smiled.

Every year, Lauren created something for them to set on the table. At least this year, he recognized the paper items as turkeys, which hadn't always been the case. But they all pretended to know exactly what Lauren had created.

"Sawyer, Lauren, Lisa, and Maddie will be over about one o'clock. Adam should be right behind them. He said the trails are a mess with the rain, but the roads down the mountain are fine," Rebecca said.

Bryan could see the mental checklist in his mother's mind and smiled. She had always juggled everything beautifully. She had raised four kids, served on multiple town committees, and managed the library for years. Bryan had never seen her forget anything or anyone.

"Rylee is coming with her Dad at one-thirty. She said her Dad needed to run to the store and pick up a few ingredients for the yams."

"Her Dad is coming?" Bryan stopped with his juice glass halfway to his mouth.

Rebecca tucked a spare wisp of hair behind her ears. Her cheeks flushed pink. "He arrived late last night. I guess it was a surprise, but he wants to spend Thanksgiving with her. She asked if it would be all right to bring him. Of course, I couldn't say no." Rebecca said and smiled. "Hosting Jeff Harper will be the talk of Cranberry Bay."

Bryan's heart lifted with a hope bigger than he had ever dared think possible. Something must have changed with her father. He was here, in Cranberry Bay, and coming to dinner at his family's Thanksgiving. Rylee told him her father was the reason she couldn't stay in Cranberry Bay. Surely, this must mean something had changed. Something for the better.

"What can I do to help get things ready?"

Rebecca broke from her dreamy stare at some distant place on the kitchen wall. "If you'd keep any eye on the turkey and baste it I'd really appreciate it." She lowered her eyes and drew circles with her finger on the tablecloth. "Your Dad always did the turkey. He's been gone so long now, but I still miss him, especially at the holidays." Her voice took on a sad and wistful note.

Bryan reached over and touched his Mom's shoulder. "You've done a great job on your own, Mom."

Rebecca spoke, her voice soft. "I always tried hard to give your Dad a good holiday season. His childhood holidays were never happy. They were filled with his Dad's drinking."

A dark feeling jumped into Bryan's chest. He knew about his Dad's childhood. Bryan's grandfather died in a car accident on his way home from a bar when Bryan was just a baby. Dad said it was the final result of a long drinking career. But knowing what had happened didn't make his own memories of Thanksgiving with his Dad any better.

Dad had been in charge of the turkey while Mom worked on the side items. She had taught each child how to prepare the cranberry salad, peel the potatoes, and roll out the piecrust. When Sawyer turned ten, Dad said he was old enough to help with the turkey preparations. He had given Sawyer the job of basting the turkey. That year, Bryan stood at his position at the counter and rolled out a piecrust. He wanted Sawyer's very important job of filling the baster with the thick, buttery juices from the turkey pan and dribbling them over the white handkerchief placed on top of the bird. Bryan couldn't wait for the following Thanksgiving when he turned ten. He assumed it would be his turn to baste the turkey.

But the next year, Bryan had been outside, putting away his skateboard when Dad asked Adam to baste the turkey. When he protested, Dad gave him one of his hard stares and told him that if he had been in the kitchen, he would have been asked. Bryan clenched his teeth and his new braces bit into the sides of his cheeks. He vowed next year would be his turn. But by the following year, Dad had died, leaving the whole experience to be etched in Bryan's mind as a place where he just didn't measure up to his father's expectations.

Now Bryan opened the oven door and a whiff of turkey hit him. He grabbed a hot pad and pulled out the oven rack. Bryan carefully dripped the juices on top of the handkerchief. By now, he had basted the turkey more times than he could count, but he still harbored the small, unsettled feeling of not measuring up. Sometimes he expected Dad to appear into the kitchen, yank the baster from his hands, and give it to one of his brothers.

For the next couple of hours, Bryan busied himself taking care of small tasks around the home. He changed a couple of hard-to-reach lightbulbs in the ceiling, replaced the battery on the smoke alarm, and fixed a bathroom towel hook that had come loose. All the while, he was trying not to allow himself to get too carried away about Thanksgiving dinner, Rylee, and her father.

At one o'clock, Sawyer, Lauren, Lisa, and Maddie arrived in a sweep of energy and noise. Lauren danced into the kitchen and demanded she be the one to help set the table and place the turkey place cards. She wanted to seat everyone where she wanted to seat them. Rebecca mentioned there would be an extra guest, Rylee's father. Immediately, Lauren pulled out her tin of colored pencils and construction paper and began making a turkey for his place setting.

Lisa stepped into the kitchen. She carried a handful of orange-and-brown aprons. Lisa handed an apron to her mother. She helped tie the long ties across Mom's back in a neat bow. Lisa slipped on a matching full-length apron with a ruffled middle pocket. She covered up black dress slacks, a black turtleneck sweater, and a colorful red scarf with an orange fringe. Lisa's gold hoop earrings dangled from her ears and caught the light as she turned and fitted Lauren with a child-size apron made from the same fabric as Rebecca's. Lauren twirled around the room as tears gathered in the corners of Rebecca's eyes, and she quickly turned to wipe them away.

"Nice aprons, Mom." Maddie stood in the doorway. She crossed her arms.

"I have one for you too," Lisa said to her daughter. She handed her a beautiful blue-and-yellow apron, which matched another one in her hand. "Your apron matches with Rylee's. I made them from the same vintage pattern."

"Will you tie it for me?" Maddie's eyes sparkled. A small smile crossed her lips as she turned to Lisa. For a minute, no one moved as mother and daughter shared the moment. Lisa stepped forward and embraced Maddie in a large hug.

"Happy Thanksgiving!" Adam's deep voice called out as strode into the kitchen. His arms were filled with bags of cherries, cranberries, oranges, and apples. Adam placed everything on the kitchen table and walked over to give Rebecca a big bear hug. Though the youngest of the Shuster siblings, he towered over all of them. His body was strong and lean from his days working on the mountain trails and campgrounds.

By one-thirty, the house oozed with the holiday cheer. A fire crackled in the fireplace, and Lauren and Maddie played a board game. They sat on the couch with the game between them and laughed as the pieces kept falling off the board. Lisa curled in the plush oversized chair. She tucked her legs beneath her and talked to Adam, who rocked back and forth in the old rocking chair.

In the adjoining dining room, Sawyer placed glasses and silverware around the long oak table. Occasionally, he stopped to reprimand Lauren for her over-enthusiasm with the board game, as she shouted through the small, cozy rooms.

Bryan opened the oak china cabinet. Carefully, he pulled out a stack of plates.

Sawyer took the plates and said, "I saw your riverboat agenda on the City Council staff report that went out this week. I'll work on getting supporters to back the project. How is your part of the bet coming?"

Bryan opened his mouth to respond as the doorbell rang.

"I've got it!" Lauren hopped up from the couch. She spilled game pieces everywhere and danced to the door.

"Raisin!" Lauren knelt down to embrace the dog. Around his collar, he wore a festive handkerchief with turkeys printed on it.

Rylee stood in the doorway. Her long black raincoat was open over a brown knit dress with a cowl neckline. She had pulled her hair up into a knot at the back of her neck. Strands of her long hair draped down and showed off a small set of pearl earrings and a gold necklace with a seashell, both which Bryan knew she'd found at Ivy's antique shop. Her cheeks glowed pink, and her eyes sparkled. She held a loaf of bread in her hands that was covered with a red-and-white checked dishcloth. Beside her stood a tall man who wore dark jeans and a light tan sweater.

Across the room, Rylee gazed into Bryan's eyes. He didn't hear or see anyone else in the room. Immediately, he stepped toward the door as Raisin bounded away from Lauren and toward the kitchen. Lauren screamed and ran after Raisin.

"Whoa!" Sawyer called out. He grabbed his daughter's sleeve as she flew by the dining room table. "Get the dog under control."

"Sorry. I'll get Raisin." Rylee's cheeks flushed bright pink as she rushed into the room and collided with Bryan. Her body slowed, moving into his as if they had always belonged together. He reached out his arm and wrapped her lightly around her waist, and steadying her. "It's okay." He looked down at her and smiled. "Happy Thanksgiving."

"Happy Thanksgiving." Rylee's eyes sparkled at him and made him feel he could do anything.

Rebecca stepped into the room from the kitchen. She wiped her hands on her apron. Her cheeks blushed pink as she stepped forward and extended her hand to Jeff. "Welcome home to Cranberry Bay. We're so glad you could join us."

"Come on." Bryan placed his hand on Rylee's lower back. "I'll show you where to place the bread." He guided Rylee into the kitchen, where Lisa engulfed Rylee in a large hug. She pulled the last apron from the hook by the counter. "Your apron for the festivities."

Rylee thanked Lisa and placed the apron around over her head. Bryan stepped up and took the ties from her. Their fingers met, and he caressed her palm and inner wrists without saying a word.

"Come on you two." Lisa nudged Bryan. "This is a working kitchen. We've got a Thanksgiving meal to serve before everything gets too cold." She turned around and stirred a pot full of steaming mashed potatoes.

Bryan flushed at his sister's comments and, touching Rylee's shoulder, moved to the stove to pull out the turkey. In minutes, the countertop was filled with cranberries in a rich deep red sauce, steaming mashed potatoes, and a rich green salad. The turkey gleamed on the stove top with rich buttery sauces coating the skin. The family quickly formed a line, well-

161

practiced by many Thanksgivings together. Plates were filled, and everyone moved into the dining room, where great laughter followed over Lauren's festive turkey place cards and her arrangement of seating. Bryan was secretly thrilled to find himself seated next to Rylee.

Once everyone took their seats, Rebecca stood at the head of the table. She'd taken off her apron and wore a simple, black dress. It was the same dress she'd worn on holidays for as long as Bryan could remember.

Rebecca raised her glass in a toast. "On Thanksgiving, we have always had the tradition to go around the room and say one thing we are grateful for. I'd like to continue that tradition by saying that I am very grateful to have all of you home this year." She looked to the end of the table and smiled at Lisa and Maddie. Tears filled her eyes, and she quickly sat down and took a long drink of her white wine.

Seated to the left of Mom, Sawyer stood and raised his glass. "I am also especially grateful to have all of the family here. Especially my daughter, Lauren." He smiled at Lauren who grinned back at him. "But," he paused. "I am very grateful this year to have just landed a new commercial contract to build a set of three new buildings on the far edge of town."

Applause filled the room as Rebecca said, "How wonderful! This will mean new jobs in Cranberry Bay."

"Yes," Sawyer straightened his shoulders. "It's a commercial deal for a set of popular stores and will bring more options to this area, including the beach towns as well as Cranberry Bay."

"But what about our local Cranberry Bay stores?" Bryan asked and frowned. "How will these new big chain stores impact them?"

"It won't be a problem," Sawyer said smoothly. "The stores going into the new development will not compete directly with ours. The people of Cranberry Bay will still shop our smaller, local stores because it will be more convenient than driving twenty minutes south. But the addition of these stores will allow for a greater choice of goods without needing to go into Portland."

"Mmmm..." Bryan muttered, not convinced at Sawyer's words but also not wanting to squash the new development and jobs for Cranberry Bay.

"I have news too," Adam raised his glass and stood. "I have been awarded a large state grant to improve the trail system around the mountains. The grant will allow us to put in new pathways, including a couple new campgrounds. One can be developed into a place for school groups and summer camps."

Rebecca's eyes shone. "What wonderful news! The library will want to be a part of a children's camp. We can offer activities to the kids and books for them to read while they are at camp."

Lisa smiled at Rylee and stood up. "I am going to be working with Katie as the new marketing manager for both her shop and a new idea we are working on." She winked at Rylee. "But I can't say anything more than that."

"Does this mean you're staying?" Rebecca asked her daughter hopefully.

Bryan reached over and took Rylee's hand. He squeezed. He wanted her to know he hoped she was staying too.

"Yes." Lisa glanced at Maddie. "At least for awhile."

Bryan looked around the table at all his siblings and their successes; each one in his or her own way was trying to help support Cranberry Bay and bring new life back to the town.

Suddenly, Lauren jumped to her feet. "I am grateful for Rylee and..." she looked around the room and spied Raisin, lying with his head between his paws and staring up at the turkey on the table "Raisin!"

The whole table exploded into laughter as Rylee's Dad stood and cleared his throat. "I guess I am next. I am grateful," he said, raising his glass, "to old friends who open their hearts and their homes to me. And..." he looked down the table at Rylee, "for my daughter."

Rylee's ears flushed pink, but a grin crossed her face, and light shone from her eyes. Her father sat and patted her shoulder. "You're next baby girl."

Slowly, Rylee stood. Her voice shook as she said, "I am also grateful for friends who open their hearts and homes at Thanksgiving, and for those who help me work on the cottages." She smiled down the table at Maddie and raised her glass. "I am grateful to Maddie."

Maddie's face flushed with the compliment. She pushed back her chair and stood with her back straight and tall. "I am grateful to people who give me a second chance."

The connection between Maddie and Rylee was clear. In a flash of insight, Bryan realized how much Rylee had done by simply allowing Maddie to be with her, day after day, never asking any questions, never asking what had happened to lead her to Cranberry Bay. Instead, she had just accepted her and opened her heart and let her into her life.

"Bryan," his mother said. "We skipped you, but I think you're the last person to speak."

Bryan stood slowly. He looked around the table at his siblings, nieces, mother, Rylee's Dad, and his eyes finally stopped at Rylee. "I am grateful," he said simply, "for Rylee."

Rylee's ears flushed and the light shone in her smile. Bryan raised his glass to her as a solid knowing filled his heart. He loved Rylee, and he couldn't participate in the bet. He cared too much about her. He couldn't allow her to be used as a pawn. It would break her heart if she ever found out, and that was the last thing he wanted to happen. As soon as possible, he'd tell Sawyer the bet was off. He'd win the City Council's approval on his own volition and not his brother's. Then, after he had proved himself to the town, he would tell Rylee how much he still loved her.

Chapter Fifteen

The scent of evergreen drifted from the candle burning at the front counter of the New Leaf Sewing Shop. Rylee cut and measured yards of fabric for a line of customers while Lisa replaced the cloth bolts on shelves. Festive white holiday lights hung from the outside windows and cast their glow into the dark evening of the long Thanksgiving holiday shopping weekend. After a busy day, both Sasha and Ivy had finally shut their shop doors and sought comfort in the sewing shop. Both women leaned over different ends of the long table in the back of the shop and pinned their apron patterns.

Katie sorted through misplaced patterns at the file cabinet. Dark circles rimmed her eyes, but a cheerful smile broke across her face as she glanced up at the groups of shoppers walking among the fabric. There had been a steady trail of customers for the past two days, and Katie had been kept hopping with requests for holiday fabric, sign-ups for December ornament-making classes, and gift certificates.

Lisa stepped up to the counter and ran her hands through her hair. "Beth Dawson was in the shop earlier today. She asked me about our proposed vintage market." Lisa frowned. "I think we could have a problem with getting the City Council's full approval. Councilwoman Beth Dawson is head of the annual Craft Fair hosted at the high school. It's been her baby for years. She sees our vintage market as competing with her project."

"Beth Dawson?" Rylee placed a bolt of fabric in a metal bin on the edge of the counter. "She sells coffee at the highway rest stop stand?"

"Yes." Katie shut the file cabinet drawer. "She runs the Cranberry Bay Youth Program. The craft show is the biggest fund-raiser of the year for the kids."

"I met her when I stopped at the rest stop on my drive into Cranberry Bay," Rylee said. That afternoon seemed so long ago. So much had happened in the last month: friendship and laughter with the sewing circle, mentoring Maddie, repairs on her grandmother's home, her father appearing on her doorstep, and Bryan. Rylee flushed, thinking about Bryan and the way he looked at her yesterday, saying her name and announcing to everyone that he was grateful to her.

"We're going to have to come up with a plan to talk to her about our idea," Lisa said. "We don't want Beth to think we're competing with the Craft Fair, and we want her to support our idea."

"What if we combine her market with ours? We could invite the crafters from her market to exhibit at ours," Rylee suggested.

"You're right," Ivy said, her voice a little garbled by the pin she held lightly between her teeth. Ivy removed the pin from her mouth and slipped it into the place on the holiday apron fabric. "I don't see why we couldn't all work together."

"Because..." Sasha said slowly as her eyes blazed at Ivy. "I am the one who sells the goodies from the bakery. We can't have all these little homemade wrapped brownies and cookies that Beth always has at her fair." Sasha cut firmly into her fabric. "Beth doesn't even have a permit to sell food at the Craft Fair. But everyone turns a blind eye because she's on every committee in town and no one wants to cross her."

"But if we don't have Beth on board," Katie said. "Our vintage market proposal will not pass the council. We won't get a permit."

"I don't even think the council looks at the proposals," Sasha said. "They rely on Beth, who is not always right."

Ivy grimaced. "No. She's not. The time she ruled not to allow anything to be on the sidewalks of Main Street about killed all of our business that summer. The tourists stop because of the brightly colored flowerpots and sidewalk displays. But Beth decided those decorations made the street look junky and tacky. I lost about thirty percent of my walk-in business that season, as did every store along Main Street. Of course, the council never mentioned it, and the next year sidewalk displays were back."

"There has to be a way to work with her," Rylee said. "Why don't I go talk to her? I could take her a small check for her youth fund-raiser and that might sweeten the deal."

"Good luck." Sasha muttered under her breath as she stabbed her pattern with a pin. The tissue crinkled under the force. "It'll take more than a check to change Beth Dawson."

A woman carrying an armful of fabric bolts and sewing notions placed her items on the counter and motioned to Katie. Katie excused herself and strode toward the front of the shop. Her blonde hair, pulled into a ponytail, bounced on her shoulder and made her look like a perky teenage clerk instead of the owner of the shop.

Rylee's cell phone rang and she scooped it out of her bag, which was hanging from the back of a chair.

Her heart leapt as Cranberry Bay Police Department scrolled across the caller ID. "Excuse me," she mumbled and hurried quickly toward the backdoor leading to the outside.

"Hello," Rylee said breathlessly. She expected to hear Dad's voice pleading for her to bail him out of jail.

Instead, a deep male voice that she didn't recognize spoke. "Rylee Harper?"

"Yes," Rylee stepped behind a large shelf of spring fabrics at the back of the shop. "This is she."

"This is Officer Robert Anderson at the Cranberry Bay Police Department. I have a young lady with me who would like to speak to you."

"Rylee!" Maddie's voice screeched in her ear.

"Maddie. Are you all right? What happened?"

Maddie's sobs filled the phone as Rylee tried to understand the girl's jumbled words.

"Hold on," Rylee said, feeling very out of her league with Maddie. "I'm at the sewing shop. Your Mom is here too. I'll go get her."

"No." Maddie wailed, her voice filling the small phone.

Rylee moved it away from her ear.

"Please. Can you come?"

"I can come to the station," Rylee said. "But I'm not your legal guardian. I won't be able to sign anything to release you."

"Please," Maddie cried. "Just come."

Rylee pocketed her phone. Thankfully, Lisa was working at the cutting counter and helping a woman chose between two green fabrics. Rylee vowed to call Lisa as soon as she found out what was going on with Maddie.

"I need to go," Rylee said to Ivy. "Where is Sasha?"

"She left to pick up Tyler at her sister's beach place. Tyler called, and I guess there was a fight between the boys over some game. Tyler lost and wanted to go home." Ivy peered closely at her. "Is everything okay?"

"It's Maddie," Rylee lowered her voice. "She's at the police station."

"The police station!" Ivy's voice raised an octave.

"Shh..." Rylee placed her fingers to her lips, "she doesn't want me to tell Lisa. She said she only wanted to see me. I'll try to convince her to call Lisa as soon as I can. I don't know what has happened, but she was very upset."

Ivy nodded and pursed her lips. "Do you want someone to go with you?"

"It's okay," Rylee said, shaking her head. She fingered the strap of her cloth bag that she'd tossed over her shoulder. Her heart beat fast. Police stations had never been a good thing for her.

Rylee waved to Katie and headed out the back door. A light rain fell on the empty sidewalks, and Rylee pulled up her hood. Holiday lights from the shop windows glowed. Except for Lisa's sewing shop and the tavern, all of the stores had closed for the day.

Rylee quickened her pace to a half-run. She headed toward the small brick building on the edge of town. As she rounded the corner, she crashed into Bryan, who carried two cups of hot coffee.

"Whoa!" Bryan placed his hand on her lower arm. He smiled into her eyes and sent her heart cascading in her chest. "I was just coming to see you. But you're off somewhere in a hurry. Is everything okay?"

"The police station," Rylee said.

"The police station!" Bryan lowered his voice. "Is it your father?"

"No," Rylee said. Bryan was family. Maddie may not want her mother to know, but she was going to tell Bryan. "It's Maddie."

"Maddie!" Bryan straightened. An unreadable, dark expression crossed his face. "Why is Maddie at the police station?"

"I don't know." Rylee twisted her hands and bit her lip. "She called me, but she wanted to talk to me."

"Let's go." Bryan picked up her hand. Together, the two strode toward the police station. Their steps on the wet pavement matched.

Relief filled Rylee's body as Bryan walked by her side. Supporting her. Police stations brought back too many memories of the times she had sat in hard plastic chairs and waited with her mother to bail Dad out of jail. Or the times she'd gone by herself, pocketing fistfuls of cash from her waitress job. She kept cash in a mason jar under her bed, knowing she'd need it to help Dad. And it was always a matter of when, not if. To make sure there was enough in the jar, she shopped the used clothing stores and bought whatever was on sale. She always pocketed the rest in her emergency fund jar.

The front of the brick building that housed both town hall and the police station was dark. But Bryan guided her to the side. He pulled open the glass doors with Cranberry Bay Police stenciled across the glass pane in black letters. Rylee stepped inside a small office. File cabinets jammed the corners, and a computer sat on a desk. In the back of the room, sitting on a green chair, Maddie huddled under a blue blanket. Rylee stepped quickly toward her.

A tall man, wearing a blue police uniform, touched her arm. "Ma'am, can I help you?"

"It's okay, Rob," Bryan said. "We're here to see my niece, Maddie Franks."

171

Maddie lifted her eyes from the floor. Relief shone in her eyes at the sight of Rylee. But her gaze quickly darkened as she swung her head to face Bryan. Maddie scowled.

"Why did you bring him? I asked for you." Maddie buried herself deeper into the blanket. She dropped her gaze to the tiled floor.

"We bumped into each other on the street," Rylee said, kneeling beside her. "Bryan wanted to come, and…" Rylee paused, "I wanted him here." She turned and looked up at Bryan, standing beside her, and smiled gratefully into his eyes. He lightly placed his hand on her right shoulder and squeezed.

"Maddie," Officer Rob Anderson said. "Do you want to talk first or shall I?"

"Tell us what is going on," Bryan said firmly.

Maddie kicked her foot from under the blanket. She hooked it to the edge of the chair and didn't say a word.

Rylee placed her hand on Maddie's arm. A slight tremble filled Maddie's small form.

"Whatever it is," Rylee said carefully, "we won't judge you. We just want to find out what happened."

"I stole something," Maddie said without lifting her eyes from the floor. "And now I'm going to jail."

"What?" Rylee straightened and looked at the officer. "Is that true?"

"Tell her the rest," Anderson said.

Maddie raised her eyes and stared straight at Rylee. "I stole something from your house."

"What?" Why?" Rylee couldn't imagine what Maddie would steal from her grandmother's home. She'd helped Rylee pack up everything from old clothing to jewelry to kitchen items. If there was something she wanted, she could have easily asked her.

Maddie shifted her gaze and stared at a distant spot on the wall. A door opened and another officer walked in. He held Raisin on a rope leash. The dog lurched toward Rylee. Rylee grasped Raisin as he lunged at her in a bundle of wiggles and joy.

"Raisin!" Rylee exclaimed. "How did you get here?" She looked up at the officer. "Did he escape?"

The officer shook his head and nodded toward Maddie.

The room spun underneath Rylee. Raisin. Maddie tried to steal Raisin. The one thing she had depended on. Raisin, with his brown eyes and wagging tail, who was always glad to see her. He was always eager to go for a walk or a run or play with a ball.

Anderson cleared his throat. "Maddie is waiting to find out if you're going to press charges against her."

Rylee adjusted the rope leash into her left hand. Raisin leaned against her body. Every part of her screamed that she should press charges against Maddie. Maddie had tried to take her most prized possession, the one thing she'd never be able to replace if something happened. But she looked down at Maddie's slumped shoulders. Compassion filled Rylee's heart. Something was wrong. Why would Maddie try to steal Raisin? Did Maddie want to steal Raisin to harm the dog? Was there another side to Maddie that she didn't see? A low ache filled Rylee's gut, and she tried to steady her emotions.

"I need to know why. Why would you steal Raisin from me?"

"Because," Maddie looked up at her with tears shining in her eyes, "I didn't want you to leave like my Dad." Sobs wracked the girl's body, and she turned away from Rylee, pulling the blanket around her shoulders. Behind Maddie, Bryan stood quietly.

A torrent of emotion gripped Rylee as she tried to process Maddie's raw words. Slowly, Rylee steadied herself and said, "But Maddie, I'm not leaving."

"But you will." Maddie said, sobbing. "You are done with the cottage project, and you will leave. I took Raisin because I wanted you to feel like I do when everyone I love leaves me."

Straightening, Rylee looked at Bryan as a pained, dark expression filled his face. Rylee's chest constricted. She'd left him ten years ago. He had just proposed to her, and she had left without saying good-bye and had never contacted him again. She had ignored his phone calls, until he stopped calling.

Rylee picked up Maddie's hand. She entwined their fingers together. "I'm not going to press charges," she said.

Maddie poked her head out of her blanket cocoon and looked into Rylee's eyes. She slipped the blanket off her shoulders and embraced Rylee in a large bear hug. "Thank you." Her words were muffled as she buried her face against Rylee's shoulder.

Rylee gazed above Maddie's head at Bryan, and the emotion reflected in his blue eyes ripped straight into her heart. She understood the hurt she'd caused Bryan by leaving.

Chapter Sixteen

Bryan shrugged off his black jacket and hung it over a small hook along the back wall of the pub. Rain dripped down the windows of the empty room. Suzanne wiped down the front counter. Behind the bar, Tom towel-dried a thick whiskey glass and talked to Suzanne.

Bryan slipped into the hard, wooden seat of the back booth and pulled out his riverboat casino file from his black bag. Butterflies raced in his stomach, and he took a couple deep breaths. His research was solid and impeccable. The facts were clear. If they didn't do something to save Cranberry Bay, the town would become only another pass-through, used-to-be town on the way to the coast. There wasn't one person on the City Council who would argue that the town didn't need to be saved. It was just a matter of whether his idea would be the one to start the ball rolling.

The pub's front door opened, and Sawyer strode in. He shook droplets of water from his shoulders and nodded to Suzanne. Sawyer held up two fingers. Tom poured a couple of tall glasses of microbrew and handed them to Suzanne. She followed Sawyer to the back table. Bryan shook his head as Suzanne placed the beer in front of him. Suzanne gazed at Sawyer, the same attraction mirrored in her eyes Bryan had seen all his life when women looked at his older brother. Sawyer nodded to her but didn't smile. Bryan wasn't surprised.

After Sawyer's wife had died, he'd buried himself far away from ever risking his heart with anyone again.

Sawyer reached into his pocket and slipped out a twenty-dollar bill, but Bryan pushed it away. He placed his credit card on the table. "It's on me."

"Should I hold onto this for a couple more rounds?" Suzanne waved the plastic card in the air.

"No." Bryan shook his head. "City Council meeting tonight."

"Right." Suzanne nodded. "I heard it's going to be a good one. Be right back."

Sawyer picked up the glass and took a long drink of beer. He wiped his mouth with the back of his hand and frowned as he set his glass down.

"This flavor isn't as good as last month. Might have to give this a miss." He wiggled his eyebrows at Bryan. "Everything ready to go for tonight?"

"Looks like it." Bryan tapped his right finger on his file. He jiggled his foot against the floor. His knee hit the table's hard bottom in a thump, thump.

"I've talked to Councilmen Matthews and Councilmen Bickerman. Both of them are ready with their yes votes. It took a bit of persuading to convince Councilwoman Dawson, but she liked the idea of using the boats for a fund-raiser for the Community Kids Fund. I couldn't get ahold of the other two council members, but I figured you had the mayor's vote in the palm of your hand."

Bryan took a long swig of his beer and nodded. "Cole has promised me his support."

He reached into the file and pulled out the one-page bid contract between himself and Sawyer. His hands shook slightly as the words blurred.

Sawyer tapped the type on his business letterhead paper. He leaned back in the booth and crossed his

176

hands over his chest. "Looks like I'll be writing a check soon."

"I want to talk to you about the funding." Bryan swallowed.

What he was going to say would jeopardize the entire project, but he had to say it. He had no choice. He had to obtain the funding through his own means or through corporate sponsors. He needed to prove himself worthy in the eyes of the town, his family, and Rylee on his own, not on a bet with his older brother.

"Don't tell me you're pulling out?" Sawyer lowered his voice. He leaned toward Bryan.

Bryan's chest heaved. He heard his father's words in Sawyer's: Both of them always confident that without their support, he'd never succeed at anything. Bryan remembered the first time he played on the community baseball team. Dad had leaned down and said to him, "As the coach's son, the referees will look the other way at some things. You understand?" Bryan understood that day as well as he understood Sawyer's words now; Without his father and his older brother, success would elude him.

But Bryan thought it was time to prove otherwise. "I am pulling out of the bet."

Sawyer whistled. "You're calling off the bet and refusing the funding which is giving you at least three votes on the council, and it's less than thirty minutes before you walk into the meeting to present this idea? Your idea is resting on my support for passage."

"It's time I prove myself on my own worth and merit, and not on handouts from you."

Sawyer took a long swig of his beer. He traced a pair of initials with his thumb and stared hard at the carved words. "Every year, on Ginger's birthday, I sit at this table. She would have been thirty-five." He shook his head. "Thirty-five. When we were kids, it seemed like forever. Now it seems like we were robbed of all we could have been together." Sawyer's voice broke.

"I'm sorry," Bryan said, quietly. "I didn't think when I picked this table. I should have remembered..."

Sawyer looked up at Bryan, the pain etched deeply in his eyes. "You love Rylee."

Bryan swallowed hard. He had tried so hard to avoid falling in love with Rylee again. But he'd known from the minute he saw her that he still loved her. Every moment they spent together only verified what he'd known in his heart; he'd never let her go. She was his first and only love. "I don't think I ever stopped."

"I'm giving you the money for the boats," Sawyer said. "I will be your first corporate sponsor. I believe in this dream of yours, and I think it's a good one. It won't solve all of Cranberry Bay's problems, not by a long shot. The elementary school may still have to close, but it's a start, and I want to stand behind you."

"Thank you." Bryan said, knowing that the exchange of money was much more than about saving the town. It was about saving love, and he wouldn't let pride or the scars of the past get in the way of moving forward with his future.

"We're family," Sawyer said. He took the last drink of his beer. His dark eyes searched Bryan's face. "Family is there for each other, even if we don't always agree."

Bryan drained the rest of his beer and wiped his mouth. "You know, speaking of family. I'm concerned about Mom. You were right. Her health isn't good, and she won't see a doctor."

The words spilled out of him, and his shoulders lightened. For the first time since Dad had died, he felt relief. It was time to work as a family and not as one-man shows trying to outdo each other.

"Why don't we meet for breakfast tomorrow at my house with Lisa?" Sawyer asked. He glanced at his gold watch and stood. "I'll call Adam and, we will all sit down and see what we can do. Between the four of us, we could always be pretty persuasive with Mom." He gave a quick smile to Bryan. "I'm glad you said something."

"Of course," Bryan stood and reached for his coat on the small hook on the wall. "We're family."

Sawyer grinned at him as the two strode to the front of the pub. They ducked into the dark, rainy night and headed to the brick city building at the top of the street.

* * *

Five minutes later, Bryan followed Sawyer into the small meeting room. Every seat in the house was filled. A group of people lined the back wall. Sawyer squeezed his shoulder. "Go get 'em."

Bryan swallowed hard. He studied the faces of the people he'd known all his life. The town was depending on him to bring forward a new vision, a new idea for how to bring Cranberry Bay back to life. Carefully, he moved through the crowded room. He stepped over a sleeping child with a teddy bear clutched to his chest and threaded his way to the front of the room, where Cole motioned toward an empty seat. He'd tossed a dark coat over the backside, saving it for Bryan. Up in front of the room, Katie, Gracie, Ivy, and Lisa bent over a small computer. Sasha fiddled with cords. Tom Dawson stared at the overhead screen. He frowned and shook his head at the women's attempts to bring up a slideshow.

A light, familiar laugh caught Bryan in the chest. He looked up to see Rylee talking to Beth Dawson, their heads bent in conversation. Rylee smiled and tapped Beth's arm as if the two had been friends for years. Beth Dawson was one of the hardest votes to win on the council. Yet, it seemed Rylee had found a way to capture her vote for the vintage market project.

Bryan tried to push his way through the throng of people toward Rylee and Beth, but Tom Davis stepped up to the podium. He tapped a brown wooden mallet.

"Seats, everyone. We've got a full house tonight and a big docket. It looks like all of you want to see some new ideas move into Cranberry Bay."

The room exploded in applause and cheers as Bryan sat down in the saved chair. A small hand with painted nails reached down and removed a small jacket placed on the seat next to his. Rylee slipped into the chair beside his. Bryan couldn't help grin. Cole had done a great job saving him a place.

"First up," Tom said. "Katie Coos. The Vintage Holiday Market."

Katie straightened and walked to the microphone. Her full-length deep red skirt swirled around her. She wore a sparkling white V-neck top and looked as if she'd just walked off the pages of a holiday magazine. In front of Bryan, Sawyer leaned forward, his elbows on his knees.

"I'd like to propose a Holiday Vintage Market in Cranberry Bay," Katie began, her voice shaking only slightly. "Lisa is going to show you what a vintage market can look like, as well as how something like this can impact tourism."

Bryan leaned back in his seat as Lisa's colorful PowerPoint flashed on the large screen. A couple of women in the audience let out small sighs at the sight of festive booths covered with vintage lace, ribbon, and baskets. After a few minutes, Lisa and Ivy switched places at the podium. Ivy talked about how hosting a vintage market with vendors from all over the Pacific Northwest would encourage tourism rates to rise in Gracie's hotel, increase beverage and food purchases at places such as Sasha's bakery, and increase the number of people and amount of revenue coming through their small town.

Beside him, Rylee sat very still. Bryan lifted her hand and wound their fingers together. She turned and smiled. The cottages would also play nicely with the vintage markets. They could easily be used as short-term rentals for those working in the market.

Ivy explained how the old stuff of Cranberry Bay, currently tossed in her shop in a random way, could be reused and repurposed. She finished by stating that Rylee's cottage staging would be showcased in a national magazine, bringing more attention to Cranberry Bay and beginning to brand the small town as one known for its vintage appeal.

After finishing to a smattering of applause, Tom stood and asked for any opposition. Sawyer raised his hand and when called upon, asked where the market might take place. Rising to her full height, Katie stepped to the podium and announced it would be in her barn, on the edge of town, with the appropriate permitting of course. Katie's eyes flashed at Sawyer and the room hushed, no one wanting to relive the moment of a few years ago when Katie had to fight to have her store permitted, and Sawyer was the main opposition. He had a client who wanted to bulldoze the entire downtown core and bring in a series of flashy new bowling alleys. This time, Sawyer only nodded and sat down as Beth Dawson raised her hand from the seat at the council table.

"I have one question for you. Who will sell the goodies?"

Sasha scurried to the microphone. "Beth, we all love your homemade treats and know the roadside stop could not do without them. But," Sasha continued, her voice hardening. "I am the only licensed bakery in this town, and I am the one who caters events. Katie has requested my services."

Beth pursued her lips as a frown deepened between her eyes. Rylee leaned forward on her elbows, and Bryan drew small circles on her back, reassuring her.

"Come on, Beth," Tom took his place at the microphone. "We all love your treats, but you have to admit Sasha's cheesecakes are better than anything you can find in Portland or Seattle."

"Her birthday cakes are the best!" A woman near the back of the room exclaimed.

"She comes up with things at the last minute." A man in the front of the room stood and spoke without the microphone. "I was in a real bind the other day with Thanksgiving and a whole house full of guests. Sasha made up three pumpkin pies for our family gathering when our stove went out."

"Her son helps too," Jeff said from the back of the room as Sasha's face flushed. "She wants to give the young people of Cranberry Bay an opportunity to learn about business."

"The Youth Program will still sell the baked goods at the Craft Fair." Beth crossed her arms over her plump chest.

"That's fine," Sasha said, the smile evident in her voice. "We wouldn't want it any other way. We were hoping to have the vintage market at the same time as your Craft Fair. It will draw more people to both our events."

"Mmmm..." Beth Dawson said, "I can't see anything wrong with that idea."

"Good." Tom tapped the wooden gavel. "If there are no more questions or comments. I'd like to propose we take a vote for the council. All those in favor say aye."

Six voices were raised from the front table in an aye vote.

"Opposed?"

The room was silent.

"Good." Tom pounded the gravel. "The motion carries. Ladies, you have yourself a holiday vintage market. Katie, be sure to put in the proper paperwork to get the permit on your barn. We'll see what we can do about moving things along quickly for you."

Applause filled the room as the women hugged each other and quickly gathered their files and computer and returned to their seats.

"Bryan Shuster." Tom boomed. "Riverboat Proposal."

Bryan gathered his file and stepped toward the front of the room. He nodded to Cole, who was sitting at the back with his PowerPoint presentation. A drawing of the shiny riverboats, floating in the river outside of Cranberry Bay, flashed onto the screen. The room hushed and all eyes focused on the overhead screen.

"This," Bryan began, "is a new set of riverboats I'd like to purchase for Cranberry Bay." Easily he slid into his idea and outlined how the boats would improve their tourism. "It won't solve Cranberry Bay's problems overnight. But it's a start to help our tourism and revenue, and we need to build that up more."

Bryan talked through his presentation as he showed how the Riverboat Casinos could help with fund-raising, bring in new opportunities for events, and provide a boon to their local tourism economy through increased income.

"Questions?" Tom called.

"Who will fund this? Is it taxpayer money? I'm not paying any more taxes," a voice called from the back of the room.

"Corporate sponsors have been sought. Our first one," Bryan paused, "is my brother, Sawyer Shuster."

Applause erupted in the room, and Bryan knew his idea had sold.

"Any more questions?" Tom asked.

The room fell silent.

"If there are no more questions," Tom said. "Let's take a vote. All those in favor say aye."

Six voices filled the room. "Aye."

"All those opposed."

The table was silent.

"Motion carries. Cranberry Bay Riverboat Casinos is approved, and, with the proper permits submitted, can open for business in the spring. Meeting adjourned."

Bryan closed his folder and found himself engulfed by residents who slapped him on the back and congratulated him. After the crowd cleared, Bryan searched the room for Rylee. A group of people clustered around Lisa, Katie, Sasha, and Ivy. Bryan expected to see Rylee's blonde hair and hear her light laugh. But she was gone.

"Excuse me." He strode toward his sister. He touched Lisa on the shoulder and asked. "Where is Rylee?'

"I'm sorry, Bryan," Lisa said. Her eyes darkened with sympathy and compassion. "She left. She said she needed to talk to her Dad."

Bryan squared his jaw. This wasn't her fight to do alone.

Chapter Seventeen

"Dad?" Rylee walked into the living room. Warm light glowed from the stained-glass lamp, but the room was empty.

Raisin bounded off the couch with a thump. He shook himself, and she scowled at him. "You know you're not supposed to be on the couch. What's wrong with your dog bed?" She motioned toward the plush dog bed, which lay on the floor.

Raisin wagged his tail, and she rubbed behind his ears. "All right, just this once you can sleep on the couch. Where's Dad?"

The water in the bathroom upstairs coursed through the pipes as a toilet flushed. Rylee looked up at the ceiling. She softened her shoulders and smiled. The plaster hadn't been replaced, but not a drop leaked from the pipes running above her head. Jim had done his job well.

Rylee hung her jacket in the closet beside Dad's black leather coat. She ran her hand down the leather of his left sleeve. As long as she could remember, Dad had always had a leather jacket. She remembered how the coat would be the last thing Dad slipped on before escorting Mom out for a night on the town. As a child, she had enjoyed watching Mom get ready for her date night with Dad. Mom always wore silky, shiny dresses and a pretty wrap around her shoulders. She sprayed perfume on her wrists and clipped on large dangling hoop earrings. Sometimes she spritzed Rylee with the same perfume and giggled as Rylee wrinkled her nose. Mom and Dad had seemed so happy on those date nights. Yet Rylee knew that underneath the smiles and laughter lurked the constant strain and worry from Dad's gambling debts. Depending on how the evening played out, sometimes only Mom returned. Her shoulders tight with tension and all the laughter gone.

The knot tightened in Rylee's stomach as she made her way into the kitchen and turned on lights in the hallway. Dad said he had quit the gambling habit, but once the riverboats came to town, Rylee suspected it'd be too easy for him to slip down to the boats and play just one hand of cards. He'd lie, of course, the way he always did, and tell her he wasn't gambling, he was just hanging out with friends. But Rylee knew better. It wouldn't be long before Dad would be back to his old habits, and the entire town of Cranberry Bay would see what had happened to their hero.

Rylee stared out the window and clenched the counter. She had tried to talk to Dad about his gambling before. He had been on a two-day spree and hadn't come home. She called every hospital in the area, hoping that someone would tell her Dad had been admitted for a fight and was safe. An hour before her high school graduation ceremony, she slipped into her cap and gown. Dad walked into their small townhouse after she dressed. His eyes were rimmed with dark circles, a two-day growth on his face. She leapt at him. Her fists hit his solid chest, and she demanded he give up gambling.

Dad pushed her away, and she landed on the floor in a heap, her maroon gown wrapped around her legs.

"Don't you ever talk to me about my gambling," he said. "It's none of your business. Always remember that."

Stunned, Rylee could only stare as Dad walked out the door and left her to attend her high school graduation ceremony on her own. She was the only graduate in the auditorium who had no parent or aunt or uncle or grandparent to celebrate with her. She had left the next day for her summer in Cranberry Bay. She and Dad never talked about it again.

Rylee scooped a cup of dry dog food into Raisin's silver bowl and placed it before the eager dog. She sat down at the kitchen table and rested her head in her hands. Her heart pounded. She had to confront Dad. She had to tell him she was still selling Grandma's house. She needed her own life free from Dad and his debts. She'd buy her own place and restart her life. If Dad stayed in Cranberry Bay and gambled again, it wasn't her responsibility to shelter him any more. She wasn't going to help him out any more either. She would no longer take responsibility for her father's addiction. She would no longer place his needs above her own.

"Rylee." Dad strode into the kitchen. He carried his small black handbag. "I'm glad you're home. I've got some exciting news to share with you." Dad's eyes glowed as he placed his handbag on the kitchen table. He moved a paisley chair cushion to the floor before easing into the chair.

"I've got to talk to you," Rylee said. Her voice shook slightly.

Dad pulled his reading glasses from the top of his head and eyed her over the wire frames. "Everything okay with the young Bryan Shuster?"

"Yes," Rylee shook her head. "It's not about Bryan. Well," she paused. "It is, but..."

"He's a fine young man," Dad opened up his laptop. "The Shuster family always was one of the best in Cranberry Bay."

"I know," Rylee said. "But that's not really what I want to talk to you…"

"Can it wait?" Dad tapped the computer screen. "I need to take a little trip as soon as possible. I booked a midnight flight out of Portland. I've got a car coming for me in minutes." He smiled at her in that knowing way that sent Rylee's heart thumping in fear.

"I thought you were staying in Cranberry Bay?" Rylee stepped away from the table. She wanted to separate herself from her father with as much physical space as she could find. She stepped to the kitchen sink and leaned against the counter.

Dad typed into the computer and with a snap, shut the top. "You know," he stood and stretched. "I'm not sure what I was thinking. The town is just too small for me. I know your grandparents loved it here, and you seem to love it here." He winked. "But I need to be where the action is. I need to be in the heart of things."

Rylee clutched the edges of the counter to steady herself. Words bubbled to the tips of her tongue, and her nerves tingled. She had to tell Dad no. She couldn't support him any more, not at the cost of her own life. "I can't go back to Vegas."

"I know." Dad stepped up beside her. "You're going to San Diego. It's a fine place for you, and you'll do well. As soon as I take care of this investment opportunity, I'll join you. By then, the house will have sold. You'll have a new one all picked out, and you'll be into your new job."

"No," Rylee turned to face Dad. Her eyes blazed at him, and her heart pounded. "I'm selling this house and staying in Cranberry Bay."

Dad studied her. "I never realized how much you look like your Mom."

"What?" Rylee narrowed her eyes.

"You look like your Mom." Dad repeated. "She used to get this look, just like you have now." He smiled at her. "It's a good look."

"I miss her," Rylee said as tears bubbled in her throat. "So much she missed. So much I missed telling her."

"I miss her too." Dad placed his hand on her shoulders.

Tears pooled in Rylee's eyes. "We did okay, Dad."

"No." Dad shook his head. "I should have said something to you ten years ago when you came back from Cranberry Bay. You were so happy. It was the happiest I'd ever seen you. You literally glowed and walked as if there was no ground beneath you. Grandma had called, and she told me you and the Shuster boy were in love. But I was selfish. I didn't want you to leave. I couldn't imagine life without you. So I threw a game. I found a fight to be in, and I landed in jail, just so you would know how much I needed you."

Rylee took two steps away from her father. She shook her head. "You caused me to ruin my engagement with Bryan, but I could have said no to you. The truth is, I wasn't ready. I wasn't ready for what Bryan was asking. Cranberry Bay and Bryan scared me. If I married Bryan, I would become a part of this town. I wasn't ready for that."

"And you're ready now?" Dad asked.

"I think so," Rylee said. "But Dad, I can't continue to lie about you either. I can't continue to pretend. I have to tell the truth when people ask about you. You have an addiction. A gambling addiction."

Dad's eyes darkened with emotion. "It's not right to continue to lie to people."

Rylee stepped closer to her father. She smiled faintly. Her father still wasn't ready to admit to his gambling addiction. But she couldn't continue to live the lie.

From outside, a car door slammed, and Raisin barked.

"Your ride is here." Rylee picked up Dad's black bag. She followed him to the front door. Her insides felt light, as she left behind a weight she had carried for years.

In the living room, Dad turned to her. "Let me know when you're going to marry that Shuster boy. I'll be there to walk you down the aisle."

"Oh." Rylee flushed. "I don't know…"

"Yes." Dad wiggled his eyebrows at her. "You will marry him, and it won't be too much longer. I predict I'll be back in time for a summer wedding."

Dad leaned over and kissed the top of her head. Then he opened the door and walked to the driveway, where a black town car's headlights shone across the lawn.

Dad gave her a final wave and slipped into the car. Raisin nosed his head into her palm. She leaned down and buried her face in Raisin's fur, unwilling to see the car pull out of the driveway. Dad planned to get back to Cranberry Bay, but she knew how his gambling addiction worked. She might never see him again.

"Rylee!"

Startled, Rylee lifted her head as Bryan hurried up the steps.

"Is everything okay?" He kneeled down beside her and gazed into her eyes.

Dad left," Rylee said. "But yes, everything is okay."

Bryan reached out his hand. He linked his fingers with hers and helped her to a standing position.

"Why don't you come in, and I'll explain everything?" Rylee said.

* * *

An hour later, after enjoying Rylee's homemade chicken noodle soup and thick, cranberry bread, Bryan towel-dried a bowl and placed it on the counter. Rylee picked it up and their fingers touched. She smiled at him as the candle on the counter reflected the light in her eyes. Rylee had always been beautiful, but now her face reflected a new brightness, and her body moved a little bit more easily as it was finally free from the emotional confinement she had been in for years.

Bryan's conscience tugged at his chest. He never wanted to lie to Rylee. She had been bathed in lies for so long. He never wanted to see her hurt because of something he failed to tell her. She deserved so much more than half-truths, lies, and deceit. It was what she'd lived with all her life, and he wouldn't continue the pattern. Bryan folded the towel and cleared his throat.

"Rylee," he said. "There's something I need to tell you."

Rylee stepped closer to him. "Yes?"

Every part of him cried out to stop now before it was too late. He could tuck the bet with Sawyer into the recesses of his mind and forget about it. But he couldn't. There would be someone, somewhere who would tell her. He loved her too much to lie, and he had to tell her the truth, even if that truth meant she walked away from him for good.

"I haven't been honest with you about something." He looked over her head and out the darkened kitchen window.

A shadow slid over Rylee's face. She crossed her hands over her chest.

Bryan's chest hurt. He would do anything to take that look away, but he pressed forward. "When you first arrived in Cranberry Bay, Sawyer made a bet with me about you."

"A bet?" Rylee's voice sounded fragile. "About me?"

"I'm not proud of this," Bryan squared his jaw.

Rylee's mouth parted slightly, but she didn't say anything.

"I needed money to fund the riverboats. The banks wouldn't loan me anything. I had no credit history for something like the casinos." Bryan swallowed hard. "Sawyer bet me that if I could convince you to stay in Cranberry Bay, he would give me the funding for the riverboats."

"I was being used as a pawn in a bet? The time we spent together in…" Rylee's voice trailed off. The hurt was evident in her eyes.

"No." Bryan exploded suddenly. He wanted desperately to explain himself. "How I felt about you wasn't a lie. I was lying to myself. When I saw you on the highway, I told myself I wasn't still in love with you. I was lying to myself because I didn't want to feel the hurt again when you left."

Rylee's eyes softened.

"But the truth is…" Bryan said. "I never stopped loving you, and I want you to know. I tried to marry someone else and go on with my life, and it didn't work. I want you to know I have always loved you." His voice broke in the emotion of his words.

Rylee took a step toward Bryan. She ran her hand down his face. "Did you win the bet?"

"I lost," Bryan placed his hand over hers. He covered her small one with his large one. "I called it off. Sawyer agreed to fund the riverboats as a corporate sponsor."

Rylee stepped closer to him. "You won," she said quietly. "It just wasn't the bet you expected to win."

Bryan gazed down at her slightly parted mouth. He whispered against her cheek. "You're right." He placed his lips on hers. "I won the best bet of them all. I won your love."

Look for the second book in the Cranberry Bay Series in June 2016.

Please enjoy the first chapter of Mindy's Young Adult Romance, *Weaving Magic*

Chapter One

Shantel

I read the letter and stuck it in my purse. My heart pounded but there was nothing I could do about any of it right now. The best thing was to pretend nothing was wrong, just like I always did when trouble found me. I pasted a smile on my face and pulled open the screened back door of the bakery. The smell of freshly baked bread and coffee brewing always made me grateful Mia owned a bakery and not something like a fish market. I spent a lot of time at the bakery. Mia relied on me to help out when she had to be at home with baby Owen. I didn't mind so much. After I'd pop the muffins or scones into the oven, I could usually steal a few minutes to work on homework.

I grabbed an apron from the red hook by the large stove and slipped my purse under the counter. Tying the apron around my waist, I made my way to the front. Funny, there were no customers. Usually, on a Saturday morning, the bakery was packed. But before I could say anything, Mia appeared in front of me with a tray of chocolate truffles. Her dark curly hair framed her round face, and her eyes were shadowed with dark circles.

"Try one?" she asked.

"Mmm..." I took one of the chocolate balls, as the bright red painted tulip on the tray caught my eye. Mia believed tulips should be everywhere. Tulips sat in small, red and blue vases on the round bakery tables. Tulip pictures covered the walls of the bathroom—both men and women. There were even sugar cookies in the shape of tulips. Mia thought tulips were the best way to remind people the small valley town had something special to share.

Local folks knew if it weren't for the tulip festival, tourists would never stop in Riverview. They would just keep driving past on their way up to the Canadian Border. But every spring, around Easter, the annual Tulip Festival drew millions of people to the fields to snap pictures of the colorful red and yellow blooms. People crowded the shops and restaurants, and sometimes, some of them returned later in the year to enjoy a peaceful weekend strolling around the brick buildings and poking into the boutique and antique shops.

The chocolate oozed around inside my mouth and I bit back a moan. Mia never made chocolate truffles unless there was something special, like a wedding or an engagement party. She always said chocolate was too much work for a small bakery. "What's the occasion?"

"It's for... "Mia bit down on her lip and swallowed hard. Her face paled and the dark circles seemed to stand out even more.

I touched Mia's shoulder gently. I loved Mia and I never liked to see her hurting. She was only eight years older than me and more like a sister than an aunt. But Mia and I handled life very differently. Now, as her shoulders shook. I wanted to tell her to just pretend life worked out. Pretend everything was fine. Just like when we were kids, and Mia and I pretended to set up our own bakery. And look what happened. Mia owned the best bakery in town.

Wasn't it enough for chocolate candy to be delicious? Did we *really* have to talk about the reason for the chocolates? I picked up a paperback romance lying on the counter. I moved my tongue over my lips, in what I thought might pass for a slow, sensual movement the authors wrote in the romance stories I loved. I even let out a small sigh as if the chocolate was as good as a kiss. I didn't ever tell anyone that, although I am fifteen, the only kissing I ever did was at Adam's seventh grade party. And that kiss was only because Adam made a mistake in the dark and thought I was Courtney. When he found out it was me, he quickly pulled away and muttered something like, "Wrong girl," before he scrambled towards the kitchen. Mortified, I pretended Adam really did like me, and he'd just needed to run to the kitchen for a glass of water.

"I miss her," Mia said. "I know the chocolates won't bring her back. But…" She blinked back a small tear in the left corner of her eye. "I just miss her."

Stop. I wanted to reach out and shake Mia. *Just stop.* We don't have to talk about this. We can play the pretend game. My pulse pounded. We *needed* to play the pretend game. "What's this about?" I asked brightly as I flipped the pages of the paperback. "A pirate who captures a maiden? Two people who hate each other and are stranded at an inn by a snow storm? You know the last one we read was really good." Play along with the pretend game, I pleaded silently. Please. Pretend. It will all be better if we can just pretend.

Mia pulled out a tissue from her apron pocket, and blew her nose. The tissue looked pretty scruffy and I thought she could use a new one. Quickly, I turned and grabbed my purse from under the counter. I loved my bag.

I'd found the scrap material in an old costume box left outside the children's theater. 'Free' was printed in bold black letters across the top. It'd been easy to sew it together, and the purse was roomy enough to fit everything—especially my romance paperbacks.

I grabbed a bag of tissues and my tablet. I couldn't wait to show Mia how I would be reading the romances. "Look what I bought," I said as I pressed the on button. "Do you know how many romance books I can hold at one time?" I'd already loaded the reader with five romance e-books.

"I like my books," Mia said, and sniffed.

"But, this keeps what I read secret." I winked. Everyone always assumed that, as the State Science Champion of the Year, I would be reading something scientific and factual. But my favorite stories where about kind Sebastian sweeping independent and feisty Cassandra off her feet. Mia introduced me to the world of romance. It didn't take much to hook me, and I convinced Mia to form a book club that only read romance. Each month, we met at the bakery and dove into the steamy love stories. Romance book club was my favorite part of the month. I could have lived and breathed romance books. "So what are we reading this month?"

Mia wiped her eyes, and tucked the tissue back into her pocket. "I'm not sure about the title, but I think the main character is a scientist." Mia slid the chocolates off the tray onto a thin platter.

"Perfect." I'd been dreaming how, one day, my own Sebastian would walk into my life, and I'd have my happily ever after. Oh, we'd probably fight at first—isn't that what happened in all romance stories? But then, we'd see how happy we made each other, and live happily ever after.

Mia reached under the counter and pulled out a small stack of gold embossed paper cups. She sat down on a red stool, behind the counter, and began to wrap each piece of chocolate in the paper. With her left hand, Mia pushed the paper cups toward me.

"Where is everyone this morning?" The tables didn't have a single crumb or used cup on them. The tins of coffee were all still full.

"Street fair," Mia said.

"Right!" I was supposed to help at the Children's Theater Street Tent. I took a quick look at the watch on my wrist. The watch bracelet was a gift from Dad and I rarely took it off. On my thirteenth birthday, we had gone into Seattle and spent the day walking through Fremont and Wallingford looking for just the right gift. When we'd gotten home, instead of lying in bed, Mom made dinner and set the table with her special blue and gold china. That day was one of the good days.

"Shantel," Mia said softly. "If you want to talk…"

"I'm fine." I waved my hand airily at her. "You know," I said, "today could be the day when I find my happily-ever-after."

Mia only gave me one of her looks, and I grimaced at her. Finding a happily ever after was much easier than thinking about those chocolate truffles or letters.

* * *

By the time the town square clock chimed one o'clock, I was a sweaty mess and we'd run out of the stepping stones at the Children's Theater street fair tent. Both the theater's manager, Gloria, and I had been busy since the booth opened. Children and parents packed the tables and I didn't see how either one of us could leave to fetch more stones from the hardware store across town.

200

On the other side of the booth, Gloria helped a young girl insert a broken dish piece into mortar on a stone. The girl's anxious mother stood nearby. My throat closed and I quickly looked away.

Don't think about it, I admonished myself, and smiled at Gloria. Unlike Mia, Gloria would not pester me about today. Gloria and Mia had been best friends for as long as I could remember. They attended high school together, and both decided to stay in Riverview. Gloria ran the Children's Theater and always needed to raise money for the shows. Each year, Gloria thought of a different art project for kids and their parents. The projects were collected during the day and, at night, sold at a hundred dollar a plate auction. Last year, we used blank canvases people could paint. The year before Gloria found a local glass artist who was willing to teach people how to blow glass balls. Although that hadn't really worked too well, as most people wanted to keep their glass balls and not auction them off.

I lifted a stepping stone onto the table, took a step backward, and promptly crashed into a warm chest.

"Umfh," I managed. Embarrassed, I stepped away and looked up into bright blue eyes, and a face that was instantly familiar.

"Christopher," I breathed.

I could never forget Christopher. I'd met him two years ago as an eighth grader. By a strange twist of good luck, Christopher had been my partner in French. Every time he looked at me, or our hands accidentally touched, I knew he liked me. I couldn't wait until the year-end dance. I'd been dreaming about it since December. Christopher would take my hand, and lead me out to the dance floor. He'd wrap his arms around me and tell me I was the only girl for him. Of course, we'd be together forever.

But things hadn't exactly happened that way. Instead, the dance had barely started before Christopher disappeared like a magic trick. I spent most of the night trying to pretend I was having a good time when, in reality, all I could do was wonder what happened to him. It was one time when, I have to admit, the game of pretend did not work very well. When the dance ended, we all rushed outside, only to find Christopher being escorted into a police car. He could barely stand and the rumors immediately started he'd been caught using drugs. I refused to believe it. Not the Christopher I knew. He'd never use drugs.

But by the fall, Christopher was gone. Everyone said his mom had him transferred to the private high school. I had been devastated. All my dreams of being with Christopher in high school were shattered.

Now, here he was, and I could barely breathe.

"Hi," Christopher said, and smiled at me. "Good to see you." He touched my arm briefly and shivers ran up and down my insides. It was fate that we met again.

Fate.

Christopher absently picked up a spatula covered with hardened mosaic goop. "Ladies and Gentleman." He waved the pretend wand in the air.

Immediately, a small crowd gathered outside the tent. I smiled. It was just like eighth grade. Christopher was charming everyone. I stood a little taller next to him.

Christopher inserted his ungloved hand into a plastic bucket and scooped up a large handful of mortar. He rubbed the mortar over his hand. The thick gooey substance spread between his fingertips.

"Wait…I wouldn't…"

"Yes?" Christopher raised his eyebrow at me.

I giggled. Christopher looked just like our French teacher, Mrs. Pierce, who gave us a similar look when we flubbed another French word and turned it to garble. "Mortar hardens fast," I managed to say, as I grabbed a rag from the back table.

Christopher waved his hand in the air as if a hand covered with hardening mortar was all part of the show. A gaggle of giggling ten-year- old girls inched closer to him. How many other girls had Christopher entertained since I'd last seen him? Was there someone who he called a girlfriend?

"I'm a statue!" Christopher froze. He raised his hands to the sky. Out of the corner of his mouth, he whispered, "Hand me that rag." He winked at me. "I think I may have gotten myself in a mess."

Quickly, I grabbed the turpentine and cloth Gloria kept on the back table. Christopher reached out for a stepping stone and sent them crashing to the ground.

I froze.

Everyone in the tent turned to stare at us. I knew my face was turning shades of purple. I hated being the center of attention. It was okay for things like Science Fair award ceremonies where I only had to shake someone's hand and take the ribbon. But to be center stage because of something bad was unthinkable.

"I'll fix it," Christopher muttered as he leaned over and lifted the broken pieces from the ground. They were equal in size. It was as if someone had taken a knife and simply sliced down the middle. I was mesmerized by his hands and the gentle way he held the stones. What would it feel like to be in his hands, being held so gently? I shivered.

Christopher dropped a glob of mortar over one of the half-moon stones. He plunked broken slices of china into the soft white mortar. When he was finished, he held up the stone. "Two for the price of one," he said and smiled at me with a gentle, lazy, sexy look. My heart crashed to the ground like the broken pieces. Christopher had me hooked. I would have done anything he asked at that moment.

"Thanks," I mumbled.

"See you later, Sarah," Christopher said as he strolled out of the tent.

Sarah?

No, I shook my head.

He must have said Shantel.

I simply misheard.

Weaving Magic *is available in print or ebook. Please visit Mindy's website at:* www.mindyhardwick.com *to learn more about* Weaving Magic *as well as discover Mindy's other books including a novel for tweens,* Stained Glass Summer.

Best-selling author, Mindy Hardwick, enjoys writing sweet contemporary small-town romance as well as children's books which celebrate art and community in the Pacific Northwest. Her published children's and young adult books include: *Stained Glass Summer* and *Weaving Magic* as well as a digital picture book, *Finders Keepers*. Mindy can often be found walking on the Oregon Coast beaches and dreaming up new story ideas with her cocker spaniel, Stormy. Mindy loves hearing from readers and you can follow her blog to find out more about the Cranberry Bay Series and participate in fun blog hops with great giveaways: /www.mindyhardwick.wordpress.com

Made in the USA
San Bernardino, CA
19 February 2016